FETLOC...

# The U...

# Pri...

## DATE DUE

| | |
|---|---|
| MAY 1 6 2011 | |
| JUL 2 4 2012 | |
| AUG 2 1 2012 | |
| DEC - 1 2012 | |
| APR 1 7 2013 | |
| | |
| | |
| | |
| | |
| | |
| | |
| | |
| | |

D1021205

FOLLETT

LONDON BERLIN NEW YORK SYDNEY

Bloomsbury Publishing, London, Berlin and New York

First published in Great Britain in May 2010 by Bloomsbury Publishing Plc
36 Soho Square, London W1D 3QY

A CIP catalogue record of this book is available from the British Library

ISBN 978 0 7475 9931 9

**FSC**
**Mixed Sources**
Product group from well-managed
forests and other controlled sources

Cert no. SGS - COC - 2061
www.fsc.org
© 1996 Forest Stewardship Council

Typeset by Dorchester Typesetting Group Ltd
Printed in Great Britain by Clays Ltd, St Ives Plc, Bungay, Suffolk

5 7 9 10 8 6

www.bloomsbury.com

www.babette-cole.com

*To Sam and her magical hands*

# Rogues Gallery

Michael de Parrott

Lord Walter Fitznicely

Lady Sarah Fitznicely

Arabella & Antonia
Fitznicely

Fern Montecute

Count Blackdrax

Benjamin
Faulkner-Fitzpain

Penny & Patch

Ben Faloon

Tracy Fudge

Potty Smythe

Henrietta
Wellington-Green

Dominic Trelawney

Matt Khareef

Bunty Bevan

Jade Andrews

Carlos Cavello

Gilly Jumpwell

Philippa
Horsington-Charmers

Peter Fixcannon

Sam Hedges

Some of the characters
here you won't meet
until you read
The Ghostly Blinkers . . .

# Prologue

What if your perfect pony dream came true?

Just imagine what it would be like to go to an exclusive boarding school specialising in everything equestrian – with not too much ordinary school work. Do such schools exist? Well, yes, they do, but not many people know about them and the fees are very high.

Fetlocks Hall is one of them but it is not an ordinary pony school at all!

# CHAPTER ONE

# Pony School

Penny Simms helped out at the local equestrian centre, The Bevan Academy of Riding and Horse Management. Her parents could not afford riding lessons for their pony-mad daughter. Miss Bunty Bevan, the centre's proprietor, was happy for Penny to assist with the ponies after school, at weekends and during the holidays in return for teaching her to ride for only one hour once a week.

Penny loved every minute. She lived and dreamed

ponies and had a great understanding of them. Miss Bevan, who had become very fond of Penny, had taught her dressage, showjumping, cross-country riding and all aspects of horse and pony management. She had high hopes of her becoming a real star in the equestrian world one day. She often told Penny's parents how lucky they were to have such a gifted daughter. They had become very good friends thanks to the ponies.

Penny saved her pocket money every week to buy a copy of *Pony* magazine. She always picked it up from the local newsagent on Friday. One day she was walking home with her nose stuck in it, when she noticed an advertisement on the back page. It seemed to glow and jump out at her. It was an advertisement for Fetlocks Hall Pony School, describing how it was seeking children with special abilities with ponies to apply for interview as potential pupils.

She cut it out and showed it to Miss Bevan.

'Oh, that place,' she said, colouring a little. 'Yes, it's run by an old pony club friend of mine, Potty Smythe ... sorry, Portia Manning-Smythe. It's not the usual kind of pony school, you know, Penny. It's ... well, how I can explain ... other-worldly?'

Penny was curious to know what she meant by that.

'Some of what goes on there is highly secret,' said Bunty Bevan. 'If you are lucky enough to pass the entrance exam and perhaps later be selected for the Fetlocks A test, you will learn things you would not learn about horses and ponies anywhere else.'

Penny was intrigued. She made up her mind then and there to find out more about Fetlocks Hall.

Penny sent off for the school brochure. A week later it arrived in a golden envelope with a coat of arms on it consisting of a winged unicorn either side of a silver horseshoe.

Her eyes lit up as she read through the contents and looked at the glossy photographs of happy children with smart ponies. Fetlocks Hall itself looked splendid, standing majestically in its own parkland. The stable yard was Penny's ideal of how one should look. It all seemed perfect until she read how much the school fees were. Her heart fell with a thud. They were thirty thousand pounds a year!

Her parents ran a bookshop in Milton Keynes. There was enough money coming in to feed Penny and her three sisters, Charlotte, Bella and Sarah, and her little brother Oliver, but not enough for school fees like that.

Penny did not even show the brochure to her

parents. She hid it under her pillow and looked long-ingly at it every night.

Mrs Simms found it one morning when she was making the beds, and discussed it with her husband.

'If I won the lottery, the first thing I would do is send Penny there,' he sighed, 'but there's little chance of that.'

Mrs Simms gave him a hug.

However, Penny did show the brochure to Bunty Bevan, who thought for a moment and then came up with a brilliant idea.

'If you have your heart set on it and your parents agree,' she smiled, 'I can give Miss Manning-Smythe a ring and ask about scholarships to Fetlocks. I believe one is awarded each year for an exceptional student.'

'Oh, would you, Miss Bevan?' said Penny, her mind already racing around green paddocks at a full gallop.

A few days later Bunty Bevan called in to see the Simmses to talk about Penny trying for a scholarship to Fetlocks Hall.

Mr and Mrs Simms were worried.

'But it won't cost anything if I get the scholarship,' said Penny.

'It's not just that,' said Mum. 'This school is down in Dorset – that's a long way away, and we would miss you so much. Penny, you are only ten years old!'

Penny had to admit she would miss her family terribly but there would be a new family of ponies waiting at Fetlocks Hall.

'They take girls of my age,' said Penny, 'and just think how wonderful it will be when we are all together again in the holidays.'

'It's very hard to settle in to a boarding school like that, Penny,' said Dad. 'I remember being sent to one because my father was in the army and my parents had to go abroad. I was terribly homesick and lonely at times. The other children teased me about it and gave me a bad time. I had to stand up for myself. You'll have to be prepared for that.'

'Oh, come on, Dad,' said Charlotte, Penny's oldest sister. 'Gran and Grandad were miles away in Jakarta when you were at school in Oxford. Dorset's not that far away and it's not the 1970s. We have mobile phones and email now, you know!'

'Anyway, the other kids will have to be prepared for MEEE!' Penny chipped in, cantering around the living room with her plaits flying. 'I'm going to be a superstar rider and win an Olympic gold medal one day!'

'The term times seem to be very different from usual schools,' said Mr Simms.

Bunty explained that the school did a great deal of competing and these equestrian events were usually held in the summer. Winter holidays were generally longer than summer ones at Fetlocks for this very reason.

Miss Bevan reassured Mr and Mrs Simms that Penny had excellent prospects of passing the entrance exam to Fetlocks Hall but they were somewhat concerned about the small amount of time given to actual school work.

'Ah,' said Bunty Bevan, 'that's why only children who are quick learners are accepted at Fetlocks for scholarships. Penny does well in nearly every subject so she won't have a problem with that side of things. She's not only a very gifted little horsewoman, she may even become a top A student at Fetlocks.'

(She was thinking to herself what a talented child like Penny would get up to if she ever acquired the secret equestrian skills of an A student at Fetlocks. She thought it best to keep quiet about that.)

Mr and Mrs Simms looked at each other and shrugged. They knew they would not get a moment's peace unless they agreed to let Penny at least try for a scholarship.

'Well, I'm not promising anything,' said Dad, 'but there's no reason why you shouldn't have a try.'

'Yippee!' yelled Penny, jumping over Heffalump, their ancient spaniel, as he dozed in his basket.

They thanked Bunty for her help and asked if she could make enquiries.

Bunty Bevan rang her old chum Portia Manning-Smythe that very afternoon.

'Well,' said Miss Manning-Smythe, 'if this girl is as good as you say and her school can send a decent report, let's take a look at her. There is a scholarship available for the right child.'

'Topping!' said Bunty, crossing her fingers.

Everything was arranged.

As ever, Penny was full of confidence but Bunty Bevan knew that nothing is ever entirely certain with horses. She gave her extra coaching after school for the next few days as she knew Penny wanted to go to Fetlocks Hall more than anything else in the world. After all, it would be such a crushing blow if she failed the entrance exam.

Penny waited all week for a letter to come. It arrived on Saturday in the same golden envelope bearing the unicorn coat of arms.

'Letter come for Penny,' Oliver said, handing it to her.

Penny noticed he had sucked the corner. It made it quite difficult to tear open without damaging it.

'I've got the interview!' she gasped.

Charlotte was just dashing out to join her boyfriend on his new motorbike.

'Well done, Ponypen,' she smiled as she swished past, cramming a helmet over her thick curls.

'You won't want to know us if you get into a posh school like that,' said Sarah.

Bella agreed with her twin sister. They gave her a hug and wished her 'good luck'.

'Oliver come too?' slobbered Ollie.

Miss Bevan was delighted with the news.

'There are four rules for applying for the scholarship,' she explained to Penny, 'and I had to bend one of them. First, scholarship children have to be good at school work – you won't get much time to study at Fetlocks because ponies always come first. You do have to sit the usual school exams but I know you work hard at school and learn quickly. Secondly, you've got to help out on the yard with the school ponies and the pupils' ponies as well. Thirdly, you must be able to ride jolly well, so that's not a problem. Fourthly, and this is the rule I bent, your application can only be accepted if you are recommended by a former A student from Fetlocks. Now, I am not one but I've known Potty – sorry, Miss Manning-Smythe – for years and she'll take my word that you are a good bet. I've arranged everything with your present school and discussed it with your parents.

'So, madam, I'm driving you and your parents to Dorset on Tuesday. I'm sure your folks won't mind the Land Rover and my terriers!'

Penny went into a spin of delight! But then almost immediately she looked downcast.

'What's the matter, Pen?' asked Miss Bevan.

'It's my riding kit,' blushed Penny. 'Will I have to have a proper hacking jacket and jodhpurs? I've only got a hat, jodhpur boots and jeans.'

'I've explained to Miss Manning-Smythe about that,' said Bunty Bevan. 'She knows the circumstances. So don't worry.'

# CHAPTER TWO

## Instant In

**B**unty's trusty old car, a rusty red Land Rover
with Bunty Bevan at the controls, co-piloted
by Penny and packed with terriers and parents, splut-
tered through the rather shabby tall iron gates and
up the sweeping gravel drive of Fetlocks Hall.

The main house, a majestic but slightly peeling
Georgian mansion, stood on a hill in its own parkland.
On each side of the drive were neat post-and-
rail-fenced paddocks, in which grazed the most

important inhabitants of Fetlocks Hall, the ponies.

Penny's nose, pressed up against the window, was bruised as the Land Rover swerved to miss two galloping deerhounds, followed by four Jack Russell terriers. The dogs fell in behind the car, the terriers yapping excitedly. The Land Rover parked in front of the steps leading up to two great doors. Two stone winged unicorns gazed at them from their plinths on either side.

Penny bit her lip and glanced back at Mum, who took her hand and gave it a little squeeze.

It all looked very grand.

'Bunty Bevan, you old trout!' gushed a rather portly middle-aged lady in a tweed jacket and skirt, hurrying down the steps to greet them. She gave Miss Bevan a hearty slap on the back.

Bunty Bevan returned the gesture. 'Wonderful to see you again, Potty.'

'And this will be Penny and Mr and Mrs Simms,' said Potty Smythe. 'Simply spiffing of you, Bunty, to drive them down like this.'

'Penny, Mr and Mrs Simms, this is Miss Portia Manning-Smythe who owns and runs everything here,' said Miss Bevan.

'Hello. Do come in and have some tea and crumpets,' said Potty Smythe, leading them all up the steps.

Penny stopped and gazed at the stone unicorns. No, she didn't imagine it. One of them actually winked at her! Penny's mouth fell open. She pointed at it and turned towards Miss Manning-Smythe.

'It . . .' she began.

Miss Manning-Smythe, who didn't miss much, smiled at Penny with a twinkle in her eye and quickly grabbed her hand.

'Come along in now, dear,' she smiled. 'Don't mind the hounds! Then we'll have a tour of the estate. Got your hat and boots, Penny?'

Fetlocks Hall may have been a picture of crumbling elegance with its peeling paintwork and rattling windows, but the stable yard with its archway, clock tower and neat square of stone stables was a wonderful example of tidiness.

Each green stable door had a basket hanging over it, brimming with brightly coloured flowers and long trailing ivies. On each door was a polished nameplate and looking out over every door, except one, was a beautiful pony's head.

'We'll show you your quarters later,' smiled Potty Smythe.

'Oh no,' said Penny. 'I'm sleeping right here!'

Potty shot a knowing glance at Bunty Bevan.

'We'll kick on then,' said Potty, handing Penny a leather head collar and rope. 'Now go and catch that skewbald pony there in the home paddock. His name is Patchwork.'

Any nerves Penny might have had disappeared when she met Patch. Penny took the head collar and fished in her pocket for a mint. She climbed between the fence rails and walked up to him, holding the head collar and rope behind her back. With the mint in her outstretched hand, she called to the fat little brown and white pony, who lifted his head and snorted. He glanced behind him at the other ponies in the field and then turned his attention towards Penny.

'Come on, Patch,' she said. 'The others will get it first!'

Patch took another look at his friends and then charged up to Penny, who stood stock-still. She fed him the mint and neatly slipped the head collar over his nose, buckling up the headpiece on the near side.

'Good boy,' she said, giving him a pat. 'Let's go now.'

Walking by his shoulder on the same side and holding the slack of the rope in her left hand, she brought Patch up to the gate. Just then the other ponies got scent of the mint and came galloping up behind in a flurry.

'Hurry up, Patch, or we'll get squashed,' said Penny, calling, 'Gates, please,' to the little crowd of grown-ups. Potty Smythe opened the field gate and Penny walked Patch smartly through just before the other ponies caught up.

'Very neatly done,' said Potty as she closed the gate. 'He can be a bit awkward to catch but he came in like a lamb for you.'

Penny puffed out her chest as she led the pony into the empty stable bearing his name. She tied him up with the correct halter knot.

Impressed, Potty Smythe handed her a grooming kit with a dandy brush for removing the mud, a body brush and curry-comb for polishing the coat, a stable rubber for the final touches, a hoof pick for cleaning out the feet and a tin of hoof oil for conditioning them.

Penny, no stranger to any of this equipment, gave Patch a good going-over and took the tangles out of his tail with her fingers.

'You've done a good job there, Bunty,' whispered Potty, watching closely, to her old friend. 'This kid is a gem!' She turned to Penny. 'Now, dear, go over to the tack room and fetch Patch's saddle and bridle. You will see they are on the peg and rack with his name on it.'

Penny opened the tack room door. It smelt gloriously of saddle soap, metal polish, boot polish and lavender. She selected the right tack for Patch and carried it out to the stable.

'OK. Let's see if you can tack him up,' said Miss Manning-Smythe.

Penny did just as Miss Bevan had instructed her.

'Excellent!' said Potty. 'Now let's see you ride him.'

Penny nodded, adjusted the chinstrap on her hat and hopped up into the saddle.

'Come on, follow me,' said Potty, opening the gate to an empty field containing a few showjumps and cross-country fences. 'There you go, Penny. Give me your best show in walk, trot and canter with a simple three-stride change of leg across the centre somewhere. Then select a few jumps you think you can do.'

Penny rode out into the field and walked, trotted and cantered a figure of eight. Patch was a very well-schooled pony and knew exactly what to do.

She came to a halt and saluted by dropping her right hand and nodded her head for the icing on the cake. Everyone clapped! She shortened her stirrups and sat in the forward position for jumping.

'Come on, Patch,' she whispered, stroking his

brown and white neck. 'I'm relying on you to get me through this test, so let's make it look good!'

She cantered a circle and pointed him at a small crossed-pole jump to test him out. Patch loved jumping and soared over it.

'Good boy! Now for the oxer!'

Penny aimed him at a parallel bar with a small hedge in it. He flew over that.

'Now for the double! Are you with me, Patch?'

They popped neatly over two jumps with one stride in between. Penny and Patch were really enjoying themselves now and cantering towards a fallen log jump. Just then there was a distant scream and the pounding of hoofs.

A chestnut pony, ridden by a young girl with flying blonde plaits, was bolting across the field.

'Help! Help! I can't stop her!' screamed the girl.

Madly out of control, the pony was careering towards the old-fashioned iron park fencing.

'If she hits that she will be killed,' gasped Penny, glancing behind her.

She quickly turned Patch away from the log and rode him back towards the bolting pony.

Recognising Patch, the chestnut mare slowed down and Penny was able to grab the reins. The girl was almost off now and hanging on to the pony's neck.

'Grab her mane and get your head up,' shouted Penny. 'I've got her!'

The two ponies slowed down to a trot but the girl with the plaits had not taken any notice of Penny's advice and tumbled off the side, landing on her feet. Penny deftly moved the ponies away so that the girl on the ground would not be trodden on. She jumped off Patch, took both ponies' reins over their heads and ran back to the girl, who now sat screaming on the grass.

'Are you OK?' asked Penny.

''Course not, you idiot!' wailed the girl. 'I've probably broken my neck. It was all your fault I fell off!'

'JADE ANDREWS!' came the booming voice of Portia Manning-Smythe, who had seen the whole thing and knew from experience that the child was not injured. She rushed over with the other grownups. 'There is probably nothing hurt except your pride,' she continued. 'Now stand up and get back on that pony!'

The snivelling child grabbed her pony's sticky, sweat-caked reins out of Penny's hands and shuffled back into the saddle.

'I saw that, Jade,' scolded Potty Smythe. 'Lucky for you Penny stopped Firefly just in time and you fell on your feet! If she hadn't you would have been skewered on those park railings at that speed! Just say 'thank you' to Penny, please.'

Jade Andrews wiped her nose on her sleeve and looked at Penny from snake-thin little green eyes.

'I am for ever indebted,' she said sarcastically. 'Who ARE you anyway?'

'This is Penny Simms, our new scholarship girl,' said Miss Portia Manning–Smythe, 'and she has just passed her entrance exam and will be joining us at Fetlocks Hall.'

Penny's mouth dropped open.

SHE WAS IN!

# CHAPTER THREE

# The Rainbow of Stars

Penny could not believe her luck. She untacked Patch and gave him a big hug.

'I couldn't have done it without you, darling Patch,' she said, feeding him her last mint.

He crunched it up and nuzzled her ear as if he were saying, 'Well, we need children like you here.' In fact that is exactly what Patch said but Penny did not understand pony language yet.

'Well done, Penny,' said Potty Smythe. 'We will be writing to your school tomorrow with all the details. The sooner you start here the better.'

She took Bunty Bevan aside.

'Now, Bunty dear, well done for finding this excellent little girl. She is definitely A student material. Did you notice her "hands"? Superb, born not made. Just magic. Unusually gifted. She is just what we have been looking for.'

Bunty Bevan fluffed up. She was pleased with herself. She had to agree Penny did have wonderful hands. When someone rides very well and has special communication with ponies' mouths through the reins and bit, it is because they have very sympathetic hands. Penny's were more than that, as Potty Smythe had noticed. They were magical!

Mr and Mrs Simms were all enthusiasm. They were more than happy to give their permission for Penny to go to Fetlocks. They thanked Bunty and Potty profusely.

'We'll look after her here, don't you worry,' Potty assured them.

They made their farewells and as they descended the great stone steps of Fetlocks Hall a rather odd thing happened.

No, Penny did not imagine it. As she took a last look at the two stone unicorns, their eyes sparkled like diamonds and a great rainbow of stars shot out of them and formed an archway for her to walk under. Speechless, Penny stared at Potty Smythe, who winked at her and put her finger to her lips. No one else saw a thing.

As the old red Land Rover bumped down the drive, Penny turned and looked back. Standing on either side of Potty were two magnificent white unicorns, their great wings waving goodbye to her! Her heart missed a beat. But she said nothing to the others.

The headmistress walked back into the Hall flanked by her two beautiful friends. 'I know, darlings,' she said. 'She could be exactly what we have been waiting for!'

It really had been a magical day in more ways than one. Penny was so excited! She was actually going to Fetlocks Hall! All the way home she chatted to her parents and Bunty Bevan, reliving every moment. There were some things, however, she thought best to leave out. She remembered the wink and the finger pressed to the headmistress's lips. She knew that the rainbow of stars and the white unicorns were something to do with the other world of Fetlocks Hall.

She didn't know, of course, what Potty had been talking about with the unicorns but Penny suspected that there were far more secrets to be unfolded at Fetlocks Hall.

Although the excitement lasted for days, as the time of her actual departure for her new school drew near, Penny grew nervous. She remembered what her father had said about being homesick and missing his family. She sat on her bed wondering if everything would really be all right without them but she managed to pull herself round by thinking of Patch and the ponies, the unicorns, and everything strange and wonderful about Fetlocks Hall. No, this was too good to miss. Leaving her family had to take second place.

Oliver was so upset that Penny was leaving.

'Oliver come too,' he said, holding on to her leg.

'I'll be back soon, Ollie, and anyway Mummy and Daddy will bring you down to Dorset to see me. I'll teach you to ride the ponies.'

'Ollie ride ponies?'

'Yes, I won't forget.'

'Yippee!'

Her sisters helped her pack: mostly jumpers, jeans, wellies, woolly hat, gloves, socks, pants – and of course her new school uniform.

'It doesn't look as though they are very fashion-conscious at this smart school,' said Charlotte.

'Oh, she'll be back at the end of term with a plum in her mouth and a posh accent, *waaff waaffing* at us all!' added Bella.

'Excuse me, but would you mind awfully passing the salt, old girl,' mocked Sarah, putting on a posh voice. They all fell about in fits of giggles.

When her last day at home finally came, saying goodbye was awful. Charlotte gave Penny her old mobile phone so she could text or call the family whenever she liked. Bella and Sarah had saved their pocket money to buy her a pair of riding gloves as a farewell present.

Although they all wanted to come down to Dorset to see Penny settled in, Penny had decided she'd rather say goodbye to everyone at home. It would be easier than at Fetlocks. She was afraid she might cry and she did not want to do this in front of the other students or Miss Manning-Smythe.

There were many tears and a big group hug on the doorstep before loading Penny and her battered leather suitcase into Bunty Bevan's old red Land

Rover. Surrounded by Jack Russells, Penny waved goodbye madly until they rounded the bend at the end of her street.

'Penny,' said Miss Bevan as they rumbled down the motorway, being glowered at by cross people in faster cars, 'you know I told you that Fetlocks was no ordinary pony school?'

'Yes, you did say that it was "other-worldly".'

'Well, there is more to the place than meets the eye.'

Penny almost said, 'You can say that again! Most schools don't have real live unicorns in the house!' but she didn't mention it.

'I was never talented enough to be an A student there,' continued Miss Bevan, 'so I don't know much about the other-worldly side, the secrets of Fetlocks Hall. But if you are lucky enough to pass your A test you will have to be prepared for almost anything and at times be very brave. You will have to keep whatever you see and learn a secret. Even from your own family. Even from me.'

'I am good at keeping secrets,' said Penny thoughtfully, remembering the rainbow of stars and the stone unicorns that turned into real ones.

* * *

Portia Manning-Smythe took Penny's suitcase and hung her riding hat on a hook by the door. Then she and Penny stood at the top of the steps waving goodbye to Bunty as the old Land Rover rattled down the drive.

'You are not the only scholarship child here,' said Potty, 'but you are the youngest. You are going to share a room with the other two girls. Samantha Hedges is twelve years old and Philippa Horsington-Charmers is eleven. There are two scholarship boys: Carlos Cavello from Brazil, son of Don Frederico Cavello, international showjumper, and Dominic Trelawney. His dad is a famous surfer from Cornwall. Carlos is fourteen and Dom is thirteen. They are in the boys' dorm, of course.

'We do not have a house system here – we have pony clubs. Children are separated into the different pony clubs according to their specific talents. You will be in "The Valley of the White Horse". The other three clubs are "The Green Forest Tigers", "The Devil's Bridge Harriers" and "The Blackmud and Sparkling Vale".'

'The Tigers sound the most exciting,' said Penny.

'And so they are. A brave band of bold riders, the lot of them! No, it's the V.W.H. for you, my girl. They are, shall we say, more magical?'

Penny knew she was being paid a great compliment by being put in the V.W.H. She had heard of the Great White Horse cut into the chalk hills of Wiltshire. He was supposed to have special powers and had been there for thousands of years. If he had wings and a horn he would look very much like a unicorn.

The headmistress led the way up a great sweeping wooden staircase, along a balcony and down several corridors to the girls' dormitory.

Her two roommates, Samantha and Philippa, seemed really nice. Both of them had their own ponies at the school. Sam had a New Forest cross thoroughbred pony called Landsman. She was in the Tigers. Pip was in the V.W.H. and owned a dapple grey show pony called Arden Scallywag – Waggit for short.

*They must have rich parents*, thought Penny, as she unpacked a photo of her own family.

'Oh, please may we see?' said the other girls.

Pip looked downcast. 'My parents are missing,' she said. 'Mummy and Daddy went to study zebras in South Africa. They were on safari . . . and they just disappeared. Their land cruiser was found but . . .' She stopped. 'Potty . . . I mean Miss Manning-Smythe read about it in *Horse and Hound*. They were famous equine vets, you see. She took Waggit and me in. We live here for free because I'm a scholarship girl. Otherwise I'd have lost him too as there was no money to keep him. I only have an uncle in the West Indies. He's a sailor and he has no place for ponies or children.'

'Both my parents were killed in a hunting accident before I got a scholarship here,' said Sam. 'I had to go and live with my Aunt Sue then. She hates horses because of what happened. She would have sent Lannie to the knacker man if I hadn't got into Fetlocks.'

'What awful bad luck you've had,' said Penny, taking their hands. 'My life seems very easy compared to yours.'

'We really enjoy being here even though we have to work hard on the yard. But that's horses for you,' said Pip.

'We're not a bad bunch on the whole but there are one or two kids here you have to watch out for. We call them the Pony Brats,' said Sam. 'For a start there's Tracy Fudge from London, whose parents are filthy rich. She's horribly spoilt and always gets her own way. Got a little pony called Hob. Rides well, wins a lot of mounted games. She's on the Prince Philip Cup team for The Ellington, her home Pony Club.'

'Then there's The Honourable Benjamin Faulkner-Fitzpain,' added Pip. 'Very snooty. Dad's a QC and a Lord. That's a judge. The call him 'Fry 'em Fitzpain' because he sends so many people to prison. The awful Benji is a hot polo player. Very hard on his ponies. He has eight of them here.'

'Eight ponies?' said Penny, amazed.

'Yes, you need a string of eight ponies to play polo seriously. Poor things. Scholarship children have to earn their keep here on the yard, as you know. We have to mend his ponies when he's busts one up. The head, Potty Smythe as we call her, keeps a tight rein on him during term time. The ponies have to be sound before he plays again. But when they aren't here we know he has them on an anti-inflammatory drug to disguise their lameness due to the injuries they get when he's competing.'

'Then there's Jade Andrews. She's as poisonous as a nest of vipers . . .'

'You don't have to tell me about her,' said Penny. 'I've already met her. She's weird.'

'She's evil,' said Pip. 'Her pony, Firefly, is neurotic and evil at the same time, which is worse.

'Jade came back from hacking once and Firefly had spread a shoe, causing a nail to go up into her sole. She was hopping lame. Jade screamed at us for not checking her shoes before she went out but of course we had. We'd picked out Firefly's feet and oiled them just before she left so we would have noticed if she had a loose shoe or anything. She reported us to Potty but she's no fool.'

There was a knock on the door and Miss Manning-Smythe herself popped her head round.

'Getting to know each other, girls? Capital! Come on, Penny, I'll take you down to the yard to meet our head girl, Henrietta Wellington-Green, one of our most important members of staff. She'll explain your stable duties.'

Penny couldn't wait to get started. She trotted after Miss Smythe. She was going to spend most of her time looking after ponies from now on. Her dream had come true.

# CHAPTER FOUR

# The Yard

'Henry' was a tall, slim, athletic girl with long dark hair pinned neatly up into a bun underneath a man's peaked cap. She was twenty-seven years old with a degree in Equine Science and was a qualified equine therapist and veterinary nurse. She had also been a groom for the British Event Team.

Although her job was to manage the running of the stable yard at Fetlocks and oversee the other four permanent grooms, Henry was very much a 'hands-on' person. She was no stranger to the shovel and wheelbarrow. She attended to all minor ailments for the ponies under the instruction of the local vet, Peter Fitzannon, on whom she had the most awful crush! But he already had a girlfriend, the lovely Lavinia Darling, daughter of Captain Septimus and Davina Darling, masters of the Blackmud and Sparkling Vale hunt. She didn't stand a chance against that lot!

Debbie Brushforth, Angie Kemp, Pat Fairbrass and Ben Faloon, Henry's undergrooms, continually teased her about this.

'Henry, this is Penny Simms, our latest inmate,' said Miss Smythe.

Actually, Potty had already told Henry about Penny and instructed her to take special care of her.

'Henry will tell you what to do, Penny. Take your orders from her and let her know if you do not understand anything. I'll leave you in her capable hands.'

With that Potty gave Henry a hearty slap on the back, making her stagger forward a step, and strode off towards the main house.

'You've been helping out at Bunty Bevan's, haven't you, Penny?' asked Henry.

Penny nodded.

'Well then, you'll know what's what on a yard. Come on, I'll show you around.'

Penny already knew the layout of the place from her interview but Henry showed her the important areas such as the feed room with its neatly kept feed bins, stacks of scrubbed black rubber buckets, piles of feed sacks, complicated feed lists, feed supplements, bags of carrots and apples and scrupulously swept floors.

There was a walk-in cupboard full of medical supplies, bandages of all sorts, cotton wool and dressings.

A slim boy in a flat cap was emptying feed into a bin.

'Ben,' said Henry, 'meet Penny Simms, our new pupil. This is her first day at Fetlocks.'

Ben Faloon emptied the bag, wiped his hand on the seat of his breeches and offered it to Penny. He shook her hand vigorously with a bow and a wink.

'Very pleased to meet you, Your Ladyship,' he said in his soft Irish accent. 'And how old are we now?'

'Ten,' said Penny.

'Good God! They get younger every day,' he returned.

'Penny is going to help you this morning,' said

Henry. 'Take her up to the top barn and show her how to fill the hay nets. Then she can sponge out the automatic water drinkers and wash the feed buckets. I'll see you at twelve o'clock in the tack room.'

The telephone rang so Henry ran off to answer it.

'It'll be the vet,' she said.

Ben grinned. 'C'mon, Princess Penny, let's go.'

The stable yard had twenty loose boxes, a tack room, rug room, feed room, wash room for the ponies and an office. There were the usual girls' and boys' toilets. The yard was paved with old-fashioned cobblestones. You entered through a lovely archway underneath a clock tower.

The 'farm', or working part of Fetlocks Hall, with its hay, straw, storage barns and muck heap, was at the back of the stable yard. A pedestrian entrance ran from the yard through an arched alleyway that resembled a small railway tunnel.

Penny followed Ben through this into the farm-yard with its neat barns with haylofts above, a very old stone turret which turned out to be the dove house, and a curious round building known as the Ice House. This had been used before the days of refrigerators to make ice for the inhabitants of Fetlocks Hall. Now the showjumps were stored in it during the winter months.

Ben pulled open the sliding doors into a workshop. There was a quad bike parked to one side. He swung his leg over and started the bike. It had a small trailer hitched on to the back.

'Your carriage awaits, young lady,' he smiled, lifting Penny up into the trailer.

They rattled over the cobbles so hard Penny thought her plaits would fall off! They passed the lorry park where several small lorries and trailers were parked up. There were also three large wagons.

'Scannies, they are,' shouted Ben over his shoulder. 'The biggest and best lorries money can buy. The little brats that own them even have their own drivers!'

A huge blue and silver monster-sized truck with *TRACY FUDGE GAMES PONIES* written on the side in bright pink italics stood next to a sleek black and gold one with *BENJAMIN FAULKNER-FITZPAIN POLO PONIES* on it. Next along was a great flashy pink and mauve lorry with *JADE ANDREWS SHOWJUMPERS* in huge sparkling silver letters. On the back was a portrait of Jade, sitting on her pony, talking on her mobile phone!

Ben and Penny drove around the stable yard picking up empty hay nets and then went back to the barn. They climbed up a wooden ladder into the hayloft where they filled the nets with lovely sweet-smelling hay.

'Now for the hurling,' said Ben in his quiet Cork accent. He unbolted two doors that swung open to reveal the quad bike and trailer several metres below. Picking up a net, he hurled it through the doors. It landed neatly in the little trailer.

'You've got to have a good aim,' he said, 'especially once it gets a bit full.'

Penny had a go but the first three missed. The next one landed straight in the trailer.

'Bullseye!' laughed Ben.

Back in the stable yard Ben showed her how to hang up the nets at the correct height so that the ponies could not get their feet caught in them.

Penny cleaned out the automatic drinking troughs and scrubbed the morning's feed buckets with a power hose and brush.

She began to wonder if anyone actually did any school work at Fetlocks.

'Three days a week for scholarship kids,' said Ben. 'You still have to be up at six a.m. to help with the morning stable duties until eight thirty a.m., when you have breakfast. Then you start lessons at nine a.m. You must be back on the yard at four p.m. for the afternoon duties. You finish around six p.m., then supper and homework. There is never any free time or weekends off because you spend it all with the horses. The other four days a week you are full-time on the yard. Henry will give you a timetable.'

'Sounds OK to me,' grinned Penny.

It was lucky Penny picked things up quickly, otherwise there would be hardly time to learn any school work at all! On the other hand she would rather muck out than do maths.

At midday Ben took Penny back to the tack room. Henry, who was sorting out some spare bridles, turned and smiled.

'She's great,' said Ben, sticking both thumbs up.

'Thank you, Ben,' said Henry.

'See you later, Ponypen,' said Ben, tipping his cap and closing the door.

Penny wondered how he knew her nickname.

'Had fun?' asked Henry.

'Oh yes,' replied Penny.

Henry gave Penny her timetable. It was pretty much as Ben had described.

'Ready for lunch then?' said Henry.

Penny was starving.

Lunch, or 'Lunchtime Feed' as Portia Manning-Smythe called it, always took place in the main house in the refectory. This had been a banqueting hall in times long ago. It had a high ceiling, wood-panelled walls and tall draughty windows that rattled in the wind.

The walls were hung with portraits of the former inhabitants of Fetlocks Hall.

Penny was especially taken with the picture of pretty little twin girls in green velvet dresses, each riding a unicorn. A lovely lady in a gorgeous dark blue habit, also seated on a unicorn, smiled gracefully from another painting. In the next picture there was an elderly gentleman dressed as a cavalier, astride a rearing unicorn.

The funny thing was, as she passed them, the figures all waved with one hand and held a finger to their lips with the other! Penny's eyes nearly popped out of her head. She thought her hair must be standing on end.

'H-Henry,' she stuttered, 'do the pictures always do that?'

'Do what?' asked Henry.

Penny decided not to say anything, just nodded politely to each portrait and followed demurely behind Henry with her hands clasped firmly behind her back before anyone could notice.

*This is like 'Alice in Wonderland'*, thought Penny.

*It just gets curiouser and curiouser! Portraits whose figures come alive, stone unicorns that shoot stars out of their eyes, live unicorns even. What next?*

Fetlocks Hall was definitely a very strange place indeed but, far from being intimidated by these unusual happenings, Penny felt very much at home there.

'Hi, Pen!' said Sam Hedges and Pip Horsington-Charmers, joining her in the refectory queue.

Sam handed her a tray. 'Had a good morning?' she said.

'Oh yes,' Penny replied, 'the hurling was great!'

Sam and Pip looked at each other.

'Ben Faloon,' they said in unison.

Breakfast (at 5 a.m. back home in Milton Keynes) seemed a very long time ago. Penny was ravenous.

Lunch was great – all home-made by Mrs Honeybun, the resident cook. There was pea and ham soup, shepherd's pie, carrots, peas and a steaming Dorset Apple cake and custard for pudding.

Penny was very tired because she hadn't slept a wink the night before from sheer excitement.

But ponies always come first and she knew she had to help on the yard after lunch. There was no time for a nap.

\* \* \*

Meanwhile Potty Smythe and her accountant Andrew Fiddlit sat in her study with a cup of tea each and a cheese sandwich.

'It's touch and go, Portia dear,' said Fiddlit. 'I've done my best with the books but the bills are enormous. Thank heavens you've got at least three children with rich parents here. It's only their fees and patronage that keep the school going! Those three children are so ghastly, their parents don't want them at home. That's why they are paying you extra to have them here. The usual school fees excluding patronage don't bring in enough money to cover your expenses. Without this extra dosh Fetlocks Hall just can't survive. That's a fact.'

Potty Smythe groaned horribly.

'If I had my way I'd expel the three of them tomorrow,' she said.

'And bankrupt the school in the process,' added Fiddlit, taking a gulp from his cup. 'I give up!' he said. 'Horses are a big hole that just swallows money!' With that, he packed his papers into his briefcase and left.

'I don't like it,' thought Potty Smythe. 'Those Pony Brats are up to something. They are already B-plus students. If they ever become A students they are entitled to get very powerful skills. I cannot believe that any children as evil as that will use these powers for goodness. They are power-hungry little beasts just like their parents. They are spoilt, selfish, rude and cruel. What bothers me is that they seem to be hanging out a lot together recently. I would not be surprised if they are plotting something.'

Andrew Fiddlit did not know the real secrets of Fetlocks Hall. He was unaware of the magical powers A students gained and exactly how dangerous they could be in the wrong hands. Potty decided it was time to call a 'Lawn Meet' or conference of the members of the S.U.S. (Secret Unicorn Society), all former A students from Fetlocks, to warn them of the danger and put them in the picture.

After lunch Penny, Pip and Sam were cleaning tack with Henry.

Penny neatly crossed the throat latch on a bridle and hung it on a peg named 'Shanballymore'.

'That's one of Benjamin Faulkner-Fitzpain's ponies,' said Henry, who was polishing his boots at that moment.

'Why doesn't he clean his own tack?' asked Penny.

'Because his parents, along with the Fudges and the Andrewses, are paying extra megabucks for their rotten kids to be waited on hand and foot here,' Sam chipped in.

Henry shot her a sharp glance. 'That's enough, Sam,' she said. 'It keeps the school going and pays for your scholarships. Don't knock it!'

Just then the tack room door was kicked open and a skinny girl with short black hair dumped a load of tack at their feet.

'Hob's tied up in the wash room,' she snarled. 'Make sure one of your little lackeys washes 'im off good. I'm going for a soda.'

Tracy Fudge slammed the door and minced off towards the main house.

Penny volunteered to do Hob so Henry came with her into the wash room.

'Be careful of his back legs,' she said. 'He's a little devil. Safest thing to do is squirt him with warm water from the shower at a good distance.'

Penny did as Henry said but when she tried to squeeze the excess water out of his coat with the sweat scraper he lunged at her and cow-kicked out to the side. Henry grabbed one of his front legs and held it up with one hand, the other on his head collar so that he could not bite her bottom or kick Penny.

Between the two of them they managed to wash him down. Penny fetched his smart navy blue cooler rug with Tracy Fudge embroidered on it in red letters.

She succeeded in doing up the breast strap and the cross surcingales around his tummy without getting her head kicked off but was a bit worried about attempting the fillet string. This was supposed to go under his tail but she thought it would be safer to wait until Hob had settled down before she went so close to his hindquarters. She wished she could ask him why he was so horrible. Maybe he'd been hurt by someone before and was only defending himself in case it happened again. On the other hand it is said that pets are like their owners and Tracy Fudge was awful!

She untied the pony and led him towards his stable.

"'Ere, you!' came a sharp voice from across the yard. 'Put that fillet string under 'is tail, you clot. 'Ow do you fink 'is rug's gonna stay on if he rolls, twit face? He's been washed so he's bound to roll.'

Tracy Fudge had now joined Jade Andrews and Benjamin Faulkner-Fitzpain. They were slouching on a bench together, slurping fizzy drink out of cans. Tracy threw her empty can across the yard at Penny and Hob. It clattered across the cobbles, spooking the pony. He ran backwards, dragging Penny with him.

'Whoa! Steady, boy,' said Penny, almost in tears, but he reared up. She tripped on the can and fell over backwards, dropping the lead rope. Hob, now loose, shot off round the stable yard, kicking and bucking wildly. The Pony Brats burst out laughing.

A stable door opened and Ben Faloon strode out into the yard.

He approached the pony gently, his hand held out palm downwards. At the same time he whistled softly between his teeth.

Hob stood very still, looking at the ground and puffing through his nostrils as if he had seen a ghost. Ben calmly picked up the rope and quietly led the pony away, stroking its neck. He helped Penny up with the other hand.

'All right, Ponypen?' he smiled.

Penny nodded.

'Go and put that fillet string under the tail so. He won't hurt you now.'

Penny did as she was told. Hob seemed quite calm now.

Jade, Benjamin and Tracy looked gobsmacked.

'Luck of the Irish!' he laughed at the three sulky teenagers. 'Let me show you how to do that some time.'

He handed Penny the rope and walked beside her and Hob back to the stable.

Penny asked Ben why Hob was so mean and how

he managed to calm him so easily.

'You always have to give horses the benefit of the doubt,' said Ben, who was a great natural horseman. 'They only understand a few words of our language. They talk to us all the time but we can only decipher some of their body language and none of their words, if they have any.

'Sometimes they are trying to tell us something is wrong and because we can't hear them they "shout" at us. For example, a horse usually rears because he is trying to tell us that his back or more often his teeth are hurting. Most people will punish a horse for rearing, saying it is being naughty. They may be right as some of them do seem to have the devil in them but it is best to check. There may be a physical reason for the horse's behaviour. Wouldn't it be great if we could talk to them so? What I did to Hob was a trick my old father taught me. It distracts their attention.'

Ben's father, Willy Faloon, was a very famous racehorse trainer from Cork in Southern Ireland. There was very little he did not know about horses and he had passed all his knowledge on to his son.

By four o'clock all the ponies were fed and either turned out in the paddocks or put to bed in their stables.

Penny, Sam and Pip were sweeping the feed room floor and washing out feed buckets when Potty Smythe popped her head round the door.

'Hello, girls,' she said, handing them a folder each. 'You've got your Fetlocks D test coming up in two weeks, so here are your study sheets. There will be a written test and a practical one. It's very easy. You know all of it already, I'm sure.'

Penny wondered how they were going to pass any exams if they only had three days' school work a week. However, when she opened her folder it was quite plain that this was the equivalent of a Pony Club D test and had nothing to do with school work at all! Penny had already passed her D, C and C-plus Pony Club tests so she felt confident the Fetlocks Hall test would be fine.

'It's been a long day for you all so off you go for tea once you've finished out here,' continued the headmistress.

With that Potty closed the door and left.

'It doesn't look too bad,' said Penny, studying the details of the test in the folder.

'You wait until the B test,' said Sam. 'That's quite difficult. And hardly any people go on to take the A test, but if you pass you become a member of the elite S.U.S.'

'What does that stand for?' asked Penny.

'Secret Unicorn Society,' replied Pip.

'Meaning?' asked Penny.

'No one knows. It's a secret. Anyone who gets in by passing the A test is sworn to secrecy.'

'Trouble is,' continued Sam, 'Jade, Benjamin and Tracy are already B-plus students. They will be taking their A tests next year. Members – or Apostles of the S.U.S. as they are known – are supposed to be very powerful. That could be a dangerous thing in the hands of people like them. What's more, they seem to be inseparable these days, always holding secret meetings in their lorries and looking very smug.'

This worried Penny. The Pony Brats were obviously up to something. She was also intrigued about these special powers. How did A students get them?

She was dying to find out more about the S.U.S.

# CHAPTER FIVE

# The Lawn Meet

By the end of her first week at Fetlocks Hall Penny had adapted to the routine of stable work and school work. The credit had run out on the phone Charlotte had given her so she emailed her parents to let them know she was fine and told them all about her new friends, the ponies, the friendly staff, and how much she was enjoying school. She particularly liked rosy-cheeked Mrs Dogberry, the school matron.

She wanted to reassure them that their decision to let her come to Fetlocks had been a good one.

She longed to tell them the more exciting news like visions of unicorns, three dangerous Pony Brats about to become members of a powerful secret society and portraits of dead people that waved at you from their pictures on the walls, but she knew she had better keep that a secret. They would probably have thought she had gone mad from homesickness and come straight down to Dorset to take her away.

Things just got stranger and stranger.

The night after she emailed her parents, Penny woke up desperately needing the bathroom. As she was fumbling her way back from the loo along the dark draughty corridors of Fetlocks Hall she took a wrong turn, and ended up on the landing above the great hall. A flash of headlights and a swish of tyres on the gravel drive outside stopped her in her tracks.

She ducked behind a tapestry only to find a hole in it big enough for her face to poke through. The hole was where a Turk's head had once been as part of the tapestry picture. It appeared, from the other side, as if her face had taken the place of his. The Turk (Penny) was holding the reins of an Arabian horse.

It was the perfect hiding place, and allowed her to see everything that was going on.

More headlights. More cars.

The great hall was lit only by candles but Penny could clearly see Potty Smythe opening the door to the guests. Her heart missed a beat.

She recognised Mark Tory, world champion three-day event rider, Amanda Cook, international dressage star, Frankie Fastrack, the rider of Derby winners, and many more famous equestrian stars. What were they doing at Fetlocks Hall in the middle of the night? Was this some kind of party?

'This way, chaps,' Potty blustered, issuing them into the staffroom where some members of the school equestrian staff were gathered holding glasses in one hand and a plate of nibbles in the other.

Once everybody was assembled, the door of the staffroom was firmly shut and bolted from the inside.

Penny's curiosity got the better of her. She padded softly down the stairs and across the great hall, and tried to spy through the staffroom keyhole.

A voice behind her made her start! She stepped behind a suit of armour as a beautiful lady with long flowing hair, an old gentleman dressed as a cavalier and two little twin girls in long green velvet habits floated into the room. They were hovering about half a metre from the stone floor!

'Oh, do keep up, Walter,' said the beautiful lady. The old gentleman was adjusting his large hat in a mirror.

'Coming, my dear. They always wait for us.'

Penny gasped as she recognised them from their portraits in the refectory. They were obviously ghosts but as alive and kicking as everybody else! They wafted straight through the staffroom door.

Behind the suit of armour, Penny leant back against the wall to catch her breath. A small knob about the size of a marble stuck into her shoulder. She pushed it and a tiny shutter slid to the side, revealing a small peephole into the room. She could not believe her luck.

Portia Manning-Smythe was calling the meeting to attention.

'My dear and honoured guests, Apostles of the Secret Unicorn Society,' she began.

'I have called this extraordinary Lawn Meet as there are dark clouds gathering above our world, Terrestequinus. Fetlocks Hall itself is in grave danger.'

She reached under the desk and pulled out a large silver book studded with diamonds.

Her audience all rose and then dropped to one knee, bowing their heads.

She opened the book at a marked page. A great silver glare and a rainbow of stars shot out of it. Potty fumbled in her handbag for her sunglasses.

'That's better,' she said, seating them on the end of her nose. 'In the Epistles of Equitopia, volume 14, page 197, it says that on the planet Terrestequinus, known as Earth, King Valentine Silverwings of Equitopia foresees a Devliped uprising led by King Despot Dragontail of Devlipeditos.'

Potty looked up from the book and continued.

'I have been informed by King Valentine that the Devlipeds are planning to infiltrate our world of Terrestequinus this year and steal our ponies' souls. Terrestequines are easily led. If the Devlipeds invade and persuade them to follow their evil ways, or even worse breed with them, we will be overrun with nasty little ponies. Not only will our children be in danger of owning or riding a part Devliped, but if the Terrestequines join with the Devlipeds, the unicorns will be outnumbered. Then the wicked things plan to overthrow Equitopia!

'As we all know Equitopia, home of the unicorns, is where the magical scales, the Equilibrium of Goodness, are kept. The unicorns are the guardians of these scales and ensure they are always balanced in favour of goodness. The Devlipeds are planning to steal the scales. If Equitopia is conquered, the Devlipeds will control the scales and . . . well, all hell will be let loose!

'I am told by our intelligence agents, the Fitznicely twins' (the two ghostly little girls hovered above the audience so as to be seen), 'that the Devlipeds are already at work among us. They suspect that the Devlipeds have three of our potential A students on their side already.'

The audience let out a huge gasp.

'Is there any hope?' asked Derek Batram, show-jumping instructor at Fetlocks.

'Yes, there is a chance,' continued the head-mistress, turning to another page. 'King Valentine Silverwings has predicted that help will come in the form of a special child. The little girl is a Unicorn Princess and once an Apostle of the S.U.S. she will acquire the magical knowledge she needs to save our ponies from the dastardly Devlipeds' invasion.'

The audience whispered among themselves.

'I have great news for you all,' Potty Smythe continued. 'A child has recently arrived at Fetlocks. All the signs are there. Perhaps she is what we have been waiting for. She will have to be tested, of course. I have to be sure this child, Penny Simms, is a true Unicorn Princess and not a hoax. She could have been sent by the Devlipeds as a spy!'

Penny went very cold and felt sick.

It was all coming together now: Bunty Bevan trying to explain the 'other-worldliness' of Fetlocks Hall. The rainbow of stars. The stone unicorns. The portraits in the refectory.

Ben saying some ponies had the devil in them.

Could it be that the three students under Devliped influence were Jade Andrews, Tracy Fudge and Benjamin Faulkner-Fitzpain? After all, they were the only ones taking the A test next year.

Penny wanted to burst into the room and say, 'I'm not a spy! If I am a Unicorn Princess, give me the test now!' But she was too afraid.

As the meeting seemed to be breaking up she fled from her hiding place before anyone could see her and ran back to the dormitory.

Penny shivered as she climbed back into bed. This couldn't be real – could it? She wasn't a Princess! She must be dreaming . . .

# CHAPTER SIX

# The Mystery Revealed

'Wake up, Penny, it's five to six!' Pip was shaking her. 'We're on the yard in five minutes!'

'I had the strangest dream,' said Penny, rolling over and snuggling back into her duvet.

'Snap out of it, Pen,' said Sam, pulling off Penny's bedcover.

Pip got a wet flannel and wiped it over Penny's face. It did the trick.

Moments later they were in their wellies, rushing down the back steps of the Hall towards the stable yard.

Two young boys who Penny had briefly seen during her first week at Fetlocks were carrying morning feeds out to the ponies.

'The tall, good-looking dark one is Carlos Cavello,' said Pip. 'He's from Brazil. Benjamin F-F hates him because not only is he really good at showjumping, but he has played polo since he was your age and he's jolly talented. He's fourteen but he only got his scholarship to come to Fetlocks last year. The small blond boy is Dominic Trelawney. He's thirteen years old and is from Cornwall. He does not come from a horsy background – his parents are surf instructors – but he has such balance, rhythm and muscle power that he has turned into quite a little dressage star. That's how he got his scholarship. He can make the ponies positively dance.' Pip blushed and added, 'He's so kind and understanding. When I grow up I think I would like to marry someone like Dom.'

'Oh, come on,' said Sam. 'Carlos is much better-looking!'

They all giggled.

'Good morning, young ladies,' said Henry, striding into the feed room. 'I'm glad you find something so funny. I don't. You are fifteen minutes late!'

Penny, Pip and Sam busied themselves with morning duties until 8 a.m. As it was a school day they returned to the main house, showered, changed, and were on their way down to breakfast at 8.30 a.m.

Penny hurried into the refectory, tucking her school blouse into her skirt.

She had already dismissed the events of last night as a dream and convinced herself she was just an ordinary little girl lucky enough to get a scholarship to an amazing pony school.

But it wasn't as simple as that.

As soon as she walked into the refectory the figures from the portraits all whispered, 'Good morning, Penny.'

'We saw you last night but we didn't tell,' said the twins.

'They will test you tonight, Penny,' said the lady. 'Don't be frightened – just do as you are told.'

'We went through it the same as you, my dear,' said the old gentleman. 'Nothing to worry about.'

But Penny was worried. It was now clear that last

night had not been a dream. What was this test all about? She wished she could ask the ghosts to explain but she could hardly stand there in front of the other children talking to some paintings. All they would see would be Penny Simms talking to the wall! Everyone would think she'd gone quite mad. She had too many butterflies in her stomach to eat breakfast. She downed a glass of orange juice and headed for the science laboratory and a chemistry lesson with Professor Greengas.

Potty Smythe sent Carlos to fetch Penny to her study.

There was a knock on the laboratory door and Carlos Cavello strode in. He asked the Professor if he might take Penny to see the headmistress.

Penny gulped, put her test tube in its rack, and left with Carlos.

'What's it about?' asked Penny.

'I don't know,' he said. 'I am sure Miss Manning-Smythe will explain.'

Carlos knocked on the study door and opened it for Penny, who reluctantly went in.

'Thank you, Carlos,' said the headmistress. He smiled as he closed the door behind him.

Penny stood in front of Potty Smythe with her

eyes down and her hands behind her back.

'Ah, Penny,' said Potty. 'Don't look so worried – you haven't done anything wrong. I wanted to ask you if you would like to come with me on a little adventure in Wiltshire tonight.'

Penny opened her mouth nervously but no words came out. She managed a nod.

'Capital,' said Potty Smythe. 'Please be ready at 10.30 p.m. by the front steps. I know it's unusual to leave so late but it will become clear. Everyone should be asleep by then but if someone sees you sneaking out just say you can't sleep and are going to see Matron for some cocoa. We won't be back until dawn so you are excused morning stable duties.'

'I . . .' started Penny.

'Run along now, dear,' interrupted Potty. 'I'll explain everything tonight. Oh . . . and don't mention this to anyone, not even Pip or Sarah.'

Penny was excited and nervous at the same time. She had a hunch that the 'little adventure' had something to do with what she had overheard at the Lawn Meet. After all, the people in the portraits had told her she would be tested tonight.

It was difficult to keep it a secret from her friends but she did not see any harm in telling Patch all about it. He listened intently and then nuzzled her ear with his velvety lips. He whinnied as she left. All the other ponies joined in as if to say, 'Good luck, Ponypen.'

To her surprise Penny found herself actually looking forward to her night-time adventure in Wiltshire.

Nobody saw Penny as she crept down the stairs, except, that is, for her friends from the portraits who were waiting for her in the great hall.

The little girls floated up to her excitedly.

'Hello, Penny,' they said, offering her their little white hands. 'We are Antonia and Arabella Fitznicely.'

Penny shook hands with them but couldn't feel their fingers.

'You are going to have some fun tonight!' said Antonia, one of the identical ghostly twins.

'And we have every faith in you, Penny. We wish you good luck and hope you will be returning as one of us,' added her sister Arabella. (Penny hoped they didn't mean as a ghost because that was clearly what they were!) 'We are Unicorn Princesses (retired, of course,) and so is our mother.'

The beautiful lady glided over.

'I am Lady Sarah Fitznicely,' she said. 'Should you pass your test, my husband, Lord Walter Fitznicely, and I would be very pleased to welcome you as one of the family, my dear.'

The old gentleman glided down from his portrait and picked Penny up. He didn't feel of anything either.

'If you ever need our help just twist that wooden unicorn on the banister at the bottom of the stairs round to the right and we'll be right there. Go with Aunt Portia now. We'll see you later,' he added.

He floated down the steps, carrying Penny in his arms, and placed her in the front seat of Potty Smythe's Land Rover.

'Thanks, Walter,' said Potty. 'You've certainly made a hit with the Fitznicelys,' she added, smiling at Penny.

The moon was so bright that night you could see for miles. There seemed to be more stars than usual. In fact Penny had never seen so many.

'I want to explain a few things, Penny,' said Potty Smythe as she drove through the moonlit lanes towards the main road. 'You have obviously noticed that you are a "special child" at Fetlocks because sometimes you can see things that other children cannot see. Fetlocks Hall is not an ordinary school. It specialises in finding and producing children with special pony powers. Sometimes, once every hundred years, a child will be born with magical pony powers. I believe you could be such a person. Tonight we are going to find out for sure.'

'I have a confession to make,' interrupted Penny. 'I was there . . . at the Lawn Meet. It was an accident. I got lost in the corridors . . . and . . . well, I've got an idea of what's going on with the unicorns and those dangerous Devlipeds and everything.'

Potty Smythe shot her a huge grin.

'Well,' she said, 'maybe it wasn't quite the accident you thought it was.'

'I'd like to know more about the history of Equitopia and Devlipeditos,' returned Penny. 'I don't really understand how it all came about.'

'Once upon a time, long, long ago,' began Potty, 'Terrestequinus, or Earth as you know it, was hit by a meteorite from outer space. It made a big hole in a bog which happened to be the sky of Devlipeditos. The Devlipeds had been sealed underground until then, but now they got out and started causing trouble. King Valentine Silverwings, King of the Unicorns, had the hole resealed but recently they seem to have escaped again.

'The Unicorns are in charge of keeping a magical pair of scales called the Equilibrium of Goodness in balance. Otherwise there would be more evil in the world than good. The Devlipeds are plotting to steal the scales by overthrowing the unicorns, who at present outnumber them. The Devlipeds plan to get our ponies on their side to help them do this. If the Devlipeds, who thrive on evil, get hold of the scales, they will alter the balance in their favour and the world will become a very nasty place for us all!'

Penny swallowed hard. 'But where exactly do I fit in?' she asked.

'If you are a chosen Unicorn Princess you will be able to influence our ponies because one of your powers will be the art of Equalese. You will be able to speak to ponies in their own language and put them on their guard.'

Penny gasped. This was true magic indeed.

'We know that the Devlipeds can nominate their own Devliped Princes and Princesses from our A students at Fetlocks Hall,' continued Potty. 'I very much fear that three of our students are in league with the Devli—'

'You don't mean the Pony Brats – er, Jade, Benjamin and Tracy? I've wondered about them too,' said Penny. 'That means they will be able to speak Equalese as well if they get their A tests and the Devlipeds choose them to be . . .'

'Exactly,' added Potty Smythe.

'They will have to be stopped. Goodness knows what they will say to the ponies!' exclaimed Penny.

'Especially if the Devlipeds tell them what to say!' added the headmistress. 'Arabella and Antonia Fitznicely have been keeping an eye on those three. They've been having secret meetings with the horrid things!'

Penny asked why the Pony Brats couldn't just be expelled from Fetlocks.

Potty Smythe explained that according to Equilaw, the law of unicorns, everything has to be fair, so they must have a chance to take the exam. If they chose to give up the course and leave of their own accord then that would be a different matter. This set Penny thinking.

She folded her arms.

'And what if they were persuaded to leave?'

Potty Smythe said she herself could not see anything unfair in that though the unicorns might think differently.

'However,' she continued, 'there is another way. You may be able to speak Equalese before they take their A test. Then you would have a head start on warning the ponies against listening to the Devlipeds. This could be achieved by special award.'

'How do I get the special award?' Penny asked.

'That's what we are going to find out tonight,' said Potty Smythe, 'but first you will have to pass a test. You will have to do it all alone. You will have to be very brave and listen to the instructions.'

Penny was more excited than nervous. She couldn't wait to get started.

The Land Rover swung round a bend in the road. There under the bright full moon and myriad of stars appeared a hill with a great white horse cut into the chalk of the downs.

They had arrived in Wiltshire in the Vale of the White Horse.

# CHAPTER SEVEN

# Equitopian Coronation

Penny looked down at the badge on her school blazer. It was dark blue with the very same white horse on it. Underneath it, the initials V.W.H. stood for her pony club. The Valley of the White Horse. It all seemed to be tying in.

Potty Smythe drove up a chalk track to the top of the hill. She stopped near the summit and let Penny out of the car. The White Horse was below them now.

'OK, Penny, remember what I said,' whispered Potty Smythe. 'Go down to the eye of the horse. When you get there run round it three times to the right and halfway round to the left. Then sit in the middle of the eye. If you are successful two handles will appear out of the grass. They are silver horse-shoes. Hold on to these very tightly and say, "*OPEN EQUITOPIA*." Don't be frightened. If all goes according to plan it will be great fun and you will have passed the first stage of the test.'

Penny nodded. With her heart in her mouth, she ran down to the eye. Three times round to the right and halfway round to the left. Sit on the grass in the middle of the eye. Ah! Under her hands two silver horseshoes popped up like handles. She seized them and closed her eyes.

'*OPEN, EQUITOPIA.*'

Nothing happened. Penny was beginning to wonder if she had done the right thing.

Then, as she sat there, cross-legged on the grass circle in the chalk outline, the ground started to shake. Gently, like a huge dustbin lid, the eye moved upwards. It hovered in the air for a few moments, then moved sideways only to lower itself to the ground some distance away.

A bright shaft of silvery light sparkling with rainbow-coloured stars shot out of the cavern in the ground that the eye had exposed.

There was a distant sound of hoofbeats that grew louder and louder until it became almost deafening. The light got brighter and brighter.

And then they came – whinnying and snorting, tossing their long white manes and tails, beating their magnificent wings. Blue-white and dazzling, hundreds of unicorns – stallions, mares with foals at foot, young and old – burst out of the abyss and flew up into the sky.

Descending, they settled in a circle around Penny, where they bowed their beautiful heads, upon each of which was a golden horn.

There was a moment of silence, followed by a fanfare of trumpets.

A further shaft of silver light shone out from the cavern. Then, beating his great wings, a truly magnificent unicorn arose. He wore a beautiful golden crown and a golden and diamond sash around his white neck.

The other unicorns folded their wings and went down on one knee.

The unicorn flew over to Penny and knelt down.

'I am King Valentine Silverwings, King of the Unicorns,' he announced. 'Don't be afraid, child. Jump on to my back, just behind my wings. We are going for a ride.'

Penny could not speak. She was too overwhelmed.

King Valentine spread one of his wings on to the ground. Using a stout feather as a mounting block she hopped up on to his back. Once she was seated the King beat his wings and rose into the sky. The rest of the unicorns followed him. They circled, pinned their wings back and sped downwards back through the hole into their kingdom of Equitopia.

Down, down, down they flew, through a blazing tunnel of light.

It did not seem long before they emerged in another world through a similar eye on an identical white horse carved out of chalk on a green hill. They flew along under a bright blue sky, over rolling hills and vales studded with silver birch forests and sparkling lakes. They followed a river of stars until it fell dramatically over a giant waterfall.

Penny grasped the King's mane and kept her head up and her heels down, legs forward as he dived down the waterfall like a huge ski jump.

He slowed down, hovered and turned, then plunged through the curtain of water stars.

They arrived in a great cathedral-like crystal cavern. At the far end was a flight of stairs leading to a gold and silver throne. At the base of the stairs was a small three-legged glass stool standing inside a glittering mosaic of stars cut into the floor.

King Valentine flew up to the little stool.

'Here is your seat, child,' he said as Penny slid down from his silvery white back.

The other unicorns joined them and gathered around in a great semicircle.

'Bring the Cup of Knowledge,' summoned the King.

A crystal chalice, frothing over with a kind of mist, appeared in Penny's hand.

'Drink it all up,' said King Valentine.

Penny took a sip. It tasted of honey and elderflowers. Then she drank the rest of the golden liquid.

'Now let us see if you have acquired the magical skills of a Unicorn Princess,' said the King. 'Patch,' he called.

To her surprise Penny's friend trotted up.

'Hello, Penny,' he puffed. 'I've been here for about an hour. Cool place, isn't it?'

'Oh, Patch,' gasped Penny, 'I can understand what you are saying!'

King Valentine explained that one of the powers Unicorn Princesses gained by drinking from the Cup of Knowledge was the art of speaking Equalese. Penny had just passed the second phase.

'Now climb up on Patch's back,' he continued, 'and say "*Let's fly.*"'

As soon as she gave the command Patch rose into the air.

'Even cooler!' Patch exclaimed as they looped the loop a few times before Penny steered him back to the ground.

All the other unicorns flapped their wings to make a clapping noise.

'Well done, Penny,' said the King. 'You have passed the third part of the test.

'It is the knowledge of Equibatics. You can make ponies fly now. It will come in very useful.' He smiled. 'Now for the fourth part. Music, please!'

A magical tune filled the chamber.

'Say "*Let's dance,*"' said the King.

At Penny's command Patch, forgetting all about his short stubby little legs, performed a series of arabesques and twirls enough to put any grand prix dressage horse to shame! Again the unicorns clapped their wings.

'Passed again!' cried King Valentine. 'You now have the knowledge of Equiballet. You will be able to get any pony to dance like that.'

Patch and Penny were delighted with their performance.

'The fifth part of the test is very important,' said King Valentine, handing Penny a little silver bottle. 'This is a special gift of Unicorn Tears,' he explained. 'They have great healing powers. They will never run out, but use them sparingly.'

What happened next was quite shocking.

King Valentine swung his elegant head and cut a small nick in Patch's side with his horn!

'Ouch!' said Patch. 'That hurt!'

'One tiny drop of Unicorn Tears will heal an injury instantly when applied by a true Unicorn Princess,' said the King.

Penny opened the little silver lid and let one drop fall on the wound. It worked immediately and Patch was as good as new.

Again the flight of unicorns clapped.

'Ten out of ten!' said Valentine Silverwings. 'And now for part six.'

He stamped his right front hoof on the ground three times. Suddenly, a small golden Unicorn Horn tucked itself between the first and second button of Penny's blazer.

'That belonged to my mother, Queen Starlight,' advised King Valentine. 'When a Unicorn Princess blows it she will be able to command any hounds or wild beasts with its music. Let us see.'

He stamped the ground with a hind hoof.

Immediately a small, frightened antelope ran into the great chamber, pursued by three white tigers.

Penny put the narrow part of the horn to her lips and blew hard. She had never heard anything like it before. If music could sound like stars twinkling . . . well, that would be the nearest thing to it. All at once the tigers rolled over on their backs like kittens. The antelope tickled their bellies with its horns and they nuzzled its nose in appreciation!

The other unicorns smiled and clapped. King Valentine nodded.

'Have you any questions, my child?' he asked.

'If it please Your Majesty,' said Penny, mustering all her courage, 'I would like to see what a Devliped looks like.'

'I was hoping you would ask that,' came the reply. 'That is where the seventh and final test lies. A proper Unicorn Princess should be able to ride a Devliped.'

So far Penny had been delighted with her progress

but this stopped her in her tracks. This wasn't what she had intended. However, she could not give up now. There had never been a pony she could not ride so she puffed out her chest and said, 'I am ready, Your Majesty.'

'I don't expect you to do this without any help,' said the King. He handed her a short silver cane. 'This is the Lance of Courage. It will be your defence against evil.'

'It doesn't look very powerful,' said Penny.

'It is in the hands of a Unicorn Princess,' said the King. 'When you are in danger you will see what it can do.'

He blew a silver flame from his nostrils and a large bubble appeared.

Flying around like a hornet inside it was a funny-looking little red pony the size of a Shetland. It had cloven hoofs, no fur but red rubbery scales, and two small horn-like ears. Its tiny piggy eyes twinkled red. Flames and a good deal of black smoke shot out from its flared nostrils.

A row of upright spiky scales ran from where its mane should have been to the tip of its serpent-like tail. The tail ended in a vicious-looking fork. It glared at Penny, puffed out more smoke and swished its tail.

Penny wanted to run a mile in the opposite

direction. It was the most horrible little pony she had ever seen. However was she going to ride it?

'I hope this thing works,' she thought to herself, grasping the cane.

An opening appeared in the bubble. King Valentine motioned her to enter. Penny took a deep breath and went in, holding her cane out in front of her.

The Devliped launched itself straight at her like a torpedo.

Penny pointed the cane at its head. The cane turned into a long silver lance. Blue flashes shot from the spearhead at the end. It had a remarkable effect on the Devliped. To her relief it flopped on to the ground. The cane resumed its former shape.

She dared not take her concentration off the creature for a moment. Nor could she risk showing the thing how scared she was. Bravely, she slowly climbed on to its back and put a foot on each wing.

'So far so good,' thought Penny, seating herself securely and holding on to one of the spikes it seemed to have as a mane.

She gave it a slap with the cane and said, 'Let's fly!'

She wished she hadn't said that. The Devliped shot up into the air like a loose Catherine wheel! It careered around the bubble, bucking and twisting worse than any rodeo horse. It was also extremely hot to sit on. She was only wearing her school uniform. If she did not get off it soon she thought her knickers would catch fire!

Once it was flying more calmly, she gave it another tap with the cane and said, 'Down!'

It landed with a bump and lay quite still, smouldering inside the bubble. Penny gently dismounted and backed towards the exit, being careful to keep the cane pointed at its head. Its beady little eyes followed her every move.

As soon as she was out of the bubble, the Devliped went completely mad, somersaulting around in a cloud of black smoke.

King Valentine blew his silvery breath at the bubble and the Devliped disappeared with a pop!

A roar of applause rose up from the unicorns' wings.

King Valentine gently rubbed his nose on Penny's beaming face.

'My goodness me,' he said, 'you can certainly ride! You have passed all seven parts of the test with flying colours, Penny, because you are a true Unicorn Princess.'

She thanked His Majesty, who walked beside a triumphant Penny up the steps and seated her on the golden throne. 'Now, Penny,' he said, 'it is time to receive your special award.'

Another fanfare of trumpets sounded and a very small unicorn foal flew in, carrying a crown woven from silver unicorn hair entwined with golden strands of sunlight and moonbeams.

King Valentine Silverwings gently placed it on her head and crowned Penny Simms as the hundredth Unicorn Princess.

'Arise, Princess Penny,' he said. The newly crowned princess stood up and began her descent of the steps, holding the little silver cane in her hand with Queen Stardust's Horn tucked between her blazer buttons.

All the unicorns folded their wings, went down on one knee and lowered their lovely heads to the ground.

'Have you any more questions, Princess Penny?' asked the King as he walked by her side.

'If it please Your Majesty,' she said, 'I should like to ask if you would have any objections to my persuading the three children who are being influenced by the Devlipeds to leave Fetlocks Hall. If they pass their A tests they could become Devliped Princes and Princesses and receive equally strong powers from the Devlipeds as I now have. They may use them to get our Terrestequines on their side and to steal the magic scales you are guarding.'

King Valentine Silverwings looked concerned. He admitted he was worried that the Devlipeds would play a trick like this, but he was hoping the children would not be horrible enough to agree to help them.

Penny told him that their leaving the school would be the best way of solving the problem as time was running out and there was little chance of them being anything else but horrible anyway.

The King paced up and down looking thoughtful.

'If there is no other way,' he mused, 'persuading them to leave would be possible. But they must decide themselves. That way is the fairest. Any unfair interpretation of Equilaw would upset the balance of the Equilibrium of Goodness as well.'

'It is now my duty as a Unicorn Princess to preserve that balance,' said Penny.

'Then you have my blessing,' answered the King.

'Thank you, Your Majesty,' said Penny. 'I *will* think of a plan to get the Pony Brats to leave Fetlocks Hall as soon as possible.'

'Just one thing,' said the King. 'Your special gifts are invisible to anyone except another Unicorn Princess, unicorns and Devlipeds. They are very dangerous in the hands of anyone else, Devlipeds especially. You must keep the gifts safe. There is a special hiding place for them. It is under the third step of the entrance to Fetlocks Hall. The stone unicorns will guard them for you until you need them. That is where you shall find them.'

He swished his tail again and all the magic gifts and her crown disappeared in a little puff of stardust.

Penny felt lost without them. She would have liked to have kept the crown on at least.

'It is time to return to Terrestequinus now,' smiled King Valentine. 'You must keep everything that happened tonight a secret. Aunt Portia knows you are now a true Unicorn Princess and will do all she can to help you. The Fitznicely family, all of whom have been Unicorn Princesses – or Prince in Walter's case – will help you. They were the previous inhabitants of Fetlocks Hall many years ago. Charming people.'

He stamped his left fore hoof and Patch disappeared safely back to his stable.

'Kneel, Princess Penny,' commanded the King.

Penny did as she was told.

'*Equitopia Regina Electa est*,' he said, breathing softly upon Penny's head.

In a flash she was gone. She found herself sitting on the grass once more on top of the eye of the White Horse under the stars.

'All right, Pen?' asked Potty Smythe, putting an arm round her and helping her to her feet.

'Did I dream all that?' asked Penny, looking around her with a rather dazed stare.

'I hope not, Princess Penny,' laughed the headmistress. 'My two pet unicorns flew by just before your return and told me the good news. Well done, my girl!'

Penny slept all the way home only to wake up as the Land Rover bumped up to the front steps of Fetlocks Hall.

'Remember, not a word to anyone,' said Potty Smythe. 'Not even Pip or Sam.'

Penny put her finger to her lips and winked.

The dawn was breaking over the horizon. A pale strip of blue was visible between the great oaks that lay in Duns Copse at the end of the parkland that swept away from Fetlocks Hall. Soon the sun would be up, shining on the glorious vale and the sea beyond.

Somewhere a pony whinnied. Patch knew Penny was home.

'That was fun, wasn't it, Pen? Glad you got home safely,' he called.

She ran over to the stable yard to make sure he

was OK. On the way back to the main house she passed the lorry park. There was a curious smell of burning rubber and a strange red glow in the window of Benjamin's lorry.

Hoping no one had left the stove on in there, Penny climbed up the steps to the door.

To her amazement she heard a curious squeaky voice coming from inside.

'Of course you will get your A tests,' it said. 'Leave it up to us. Once you've passed and you are crowned Devliped Prince and Princesses you'll be able to speak Equalese and will be responsible for talking the ponies round to our way of thinking. They are fairly stupid and easily bribed. With them on our side we'll outnumber the unicorns and gain control of Equitopia and the scales! Once we can tip them in our favour . . . hee, hee, hee, just think what fun it will be when everybody is as bad as us!'

'But what's in it for us?' said a voice which Penny recognised as Tracy Fudge's.

'You will be powerful warriors,' said the voice. 'Devliped Princes and Princesses receive special powers. The power of Devlibatics will enable you to fly ponies like fighter pilots. You will be awarded Devliswords which have the power to bring down any Unicorn or Terrestequine not on our side. It's easy to kill unicorns because if wounded they cannot stop the flow of silver mercury from their veins.'

Penny's knees went weak. Stifling a little a gasp, she fell off the steps. What she was hearing was too horrible to even think about.

'What was that?' said the voice.

Penny rolled underneath the lorry and held her breath.

Benjamin opened the small door on the side of the lorry and looked around. 'No one there,' he said.

He closed the door. Penny, trembling like a jelly, resumed her position on the steps.

'You will also receive the Devlitrumpet with which you will be able to control all insects,' the voice continued. 'Imagine what fun you will have with swarms of stinging bees or mosquitoes or even locusts and spiders! Your reward for helping us will be Fetlocks Hall itself. You will be given the school to turn into an academy of naughtiness. Once we are in charge, children who do not obey Devliped rule will be sent here to be brainwashed. You can teach them every naughty trick you know. You'll be paid handsomely in Devlipounds so you will have not only power but riches beyond compare.'

'Sounds fun,' said Benjamin. 'I'll look forward to setting a swarm of bees on that Carlos toad!'

'I wouldn't mind covering that smug little cat Penny Simms with hordes of spiders,' said another voice which Penny recognised as Jade's.

'Bags I be squadron leader of the flying fighter ponies,' said Tracy Fudge.

'So what do you say?' said the squeaky voice. 'Are you with us, children?'

There was a moment of whispering between the Pony Brats.

Then Benjamin spoke up. 'You can count us in!' he said.

Penny's heart was in her mouth. She stretched up on tiptoe to look through the horsebox window. The Pony Brats were sitting around a table discussing their horrible plans. Sitting in the centre of the table was a very ugly little Devliped wearing a smouldering crown of Roman candles. She was looking at King Despot Dragontail himself, King of the Devlipeds!

The situation was now incredibly dangerous and she had proof of the Pony Brats' involvement in the Devlipeds' plot.

Somehow, one by one, Penny planned to get those three Pony Brats out of Fetlocks as soon as possible. She already had her magical gifts and the watchful Fitznicely twins to help her.

All she needed was a situation to occur so that she

could put them to good use.

She made her way back to the stable yard deep in thought. Patch was curled up in the straw in his box as if nothing had happened. Penny opened the door and knelt by his side.

The little pony opened his eyes. 'Cor, Pen, was that real last night or was I dreaming?' he said, rubbing one eye on her knee.

'It was real enough,' said Penny. 'After all, we are speaking to each other, aren't we? I'm going to tell the ponies about the Devliped plot and warn them to be on their guard. Can you get everyone up and ready for a meeting at six a.m.?'

Patch said he would do his best.

'We'll both get a couple of hours' sleep then,' said Penny. 'It's been a very long night!'

But Patch had already dozed off again. Penny walked back to the main house and fell into bed fully clothed. Sam and Pip were curled up in their duvets like squirrels. They did not stir.

# CHAPTER EIGHT

# The Case of The Miraculous Ear

As tired as she was, Penny was too excited to sleep. At 6 a.m. she went back to the stable yard before any of the other children or staff were around.

She was greeted by lots of different voices all whinnying, 'Good morning, Princess Penny.'

Penny gave a graceful curtsy and a huge giggle

went up. Anyone who could not speak Equalese would not have heard a thing as Equalese is on a much higher frequency than human speech. They would only have seen the ponies silently flaring their top lips and raising their heads.

'I've got something important to tell you,' said Penny. As she explained about the Devliped plot, the ponies stood listening with their ears pricked and their eyes bulging. 'It's OK,' continued Penny. 'I'm going to stop it happening but I'll need your help from time to time.'

They all agreed but had to confess they were very worried. Except for Hob, who laid his ears back and snapped at Waggit in the stable next door.

'I'd like to be a Devliped,' he said.

The other ponies glared at him.

Penny went into the feed room to start the morning feeds, accompanied by the usual bangs and snorts coming from the stable yard. But today she heard various voices shouting, 'Hurry up, Pen, I'm starving!', 'Go easy on that horrible cod liver oil' and 'Please can I have extra pony nuts today?'

'Thank you, Pen,' said each pony as she delivered the feeds.

Henry arrived. 'What has got into them all?' she said.

Later Penny brushed out Patch's long brown and white forelock. It had become very tousled during last night's adventure.

'Hey, Pen,' he said between mouthfuls of feed. 'When can we try out Equiballet and Equibatics? I'm dying to impress the others.'

'We might need to very soon,' said Penny.

She told him about what she had seen and heard in the lorry park early that morning. Patch nearly choked on his pony nuts.

'That's really scary!' he said. 'What are we going to do?'

'We have to work out some way of getting the Pony Brats to leave Fetlocks. Maybe I'll be lucky and I'll be able to use my gifts to get their parents to take them out of school before they sit their A tests,' said Penny.

In fact Penny did not have that long to wait.

She was just coming out of her biology class when Sam, Pip and Dom met her in the corridor.

'You'll never guess what,' said Pip. 'Carlos has had a fight with Benjamin F-F!'

'He caught him bashing the little Argentine mare over the head with a polo stick again,' added Dom. 'Carlos took it off him and clouted him with it.

**88**

Benjamin's in the infirmary with a big cut on his left ear!'

'Lord Fry 'em Fitzpain has been informed, of course, and he's on his way down here from London. Benjamin's sworn to get Carlos kicked out of school. He wants him arrested for grievous bodily harm!' said Sam.

'I wish it was Benjamin F-F for the chop. The boy's a snob and a bully. We must do something, but what?' said Dom, looking worried. 'Carlos says he'll take what's coming and he'd do it all over again because he can't stand Benjamin's cruelty to his ponies.'

Penny thought hard. This might be the chance she was waiting for to get the first Pony Brat out of Fetlocks. Already she was hatching a clever plan so she decided to pay a visit to the secret hiding place where her magic gifts were stored. During break she slipped away to the front steps. Making sure no one saw her she counted down to the third step. It suddenly sprang up as if on a hinge. The vial of Unicorn Tears flew up into her hand, making its own decision.

She made her way to the infirmary, where she found Benjamin sitting up in bed with a big bandage around his head. He was talking on his mobile to his father.

'Yes, he did bash me with a polo stick and my ear is half off! I hope you have him arrested. Yes, yes, I know you are in the middle of a huge trial but I do need you to do this, Father. OK, thanks. See you later.'

Matron was preparing a dressing for Benjamin's ear. Penny asked if she could help.

'What a nice, kind girl you are, Penny Simms,' said Matron. 'Here, you hold this kidney bowl with the new gauze while I take off the old dressing.'

While Mrs Dogberry was removing the bandage and dressing from Benjamin's head, Penny felt in her blazer pocket for the silver vial. Of course the bottle was invisible to anyone else.

She dribbled a little of the silver liquid on to the fresh gauze.

Benjamin's ear certainly was a mess. He yelled as Matron took off the dressing. She applied the new gauze and rebandaged it.

Penny wished Benjamin well and left for her geography lesson.

Later that afternoon a black Rolls-Royce swished up the drive in front of the Hall. The chauffeur got out and opened a rear door for Lord Quentin Faulkner-Fitzpain.

He was wearing an immaculate suit and polished

shoes, and had a smart haircut and a bristling moustache.

Potty Smythe was waiting at the top of the steps to greet him.

'Where's my son?' he asked coldly. 'I'm warning you, Portia. If you can't keep your brats under control I will sue you for negligence. I've already informed the police. They are on standby in case this is some kind of prank. But if this Brazilian bod has really assaulted Benjamin he'll be in major trouble. I'll see to that. I'm in the middle of a very important trial which I've had to put on hold for today. I am not the least bit pleased to keep the jury waiting while I'm running around Dorset!'

'Oh, come on, Quentin,' pouted Potty Smythe (who had once been an old school friend of his). 'I'm sure this can be sorted out amicably. Boys will be boys. You were always getting into scraps at his age.' She wagged her finger at him.

Lord Quentin strode into the infirmary.

Benjamin was really putting it on. He was lying in bed on his good side, moaning and holding his bad ear.

'Hello, Benjamin,' said his father. 'This had better be good. I was hoping to see someone locked up today but have had to rush down here instead.'

'Father,' wailed his son. 'Just get the brute that did this to me. Have HIM locked up.'

'I'll have to see the evidence first,' said the judge.

Matron took the bandage off. The ear was perfectly healed. Not a cut in sight!

'What is this nonsense!' boomed Lord Quentin.

'Terrible, isn't it?' moaned his son. 'Permanent disfigurement.'

'Benjamin, there is nothing wrong with your ear. How dare you embarrass me like this!' thundered his father. 'How can you tell such dreadful lies? What happens if this gets out? We'll have to get you home before the press hears about it. For heaven's sake, Benjamin, I have already alerted the police on your spoken evidence!' Lord Fry 'em Fitzpain turned a horrible shade of purple.

'Portia, dear old thing,' he cooed, 'for old times' sake let's keep this under wraps.'

'Perhaps,' suggested the headmistress, 'it would be better if Benjamin decided to leave Fetlocks to pursue a career in the law. He should really be at a school in London where you could keep a better eye on him.'

'Excellent idea,' agreed the judge.

'I won't stay a moment longer in this dump,' raged Benjamin, looking at his perfect ear in a mirror offered by Matron. 'There's dirty work going on here. This morning my ear was half off. They are a load of old witches!'

'Be quiet, boy!' interrupted his father. 'You have done enough damage without adding slander to your list! Come and get into the car right now. I'll send a valet for your things and a man to fetch the lorry and the ponies back to our yard at Windsor Great Park. We are leaving.'

'That was sudden. Miraculous healing!' said Matron to Potty Smythe.

'Wasn't it,' came the gleeful reply.

Penny watched from the classroom window as the big black car drove off hurriedly.

She secretly gave herself a pat on the back.

'One down, two to go,' she thought, busying herself with a map of Gibraltar.


The news of Benjamin F-F's sudden departure spread round the school like wildfire.

As Carlos walked in for supper that evening all the children stood up and cheered. Everyone was delighted that Benjamin had left, except Jade and Tracy, of course. They were suspicious that something was up. It seemed very strange that Benjamin had suddenly left before he had a chance to become a Devliped Prince and gain magical powers.

No one really knew what had happened. Even Potty Smythe wasn't sure but she suspected Penny had something to do with it!

# CHAPTER NINE

# The Fetlocks Hall Flyers

**P**enny was pleased with herself. With Benjamin out of the way the chances of defeating the Devlipeds were stronger but that still left the other two Pony Brats to get rid of.

There would have to be some brilliant ruse to get rid of Tracy Fudge and Jade Andrews.

She decided to target Tracy first.

Tracy Fudge had to be the best at everything, even being nasty. If she was ever beaten at anything she simply threw her dummy out of the pram and gave up. Penny remembered how she had once beaten her in a school spelling test. Tracy tore up all her notes, stormed out of the classroom and refused to take part in any more school quizzes. It suddenly occurred to Penny that this was the obvious way to get rid of Tracy! She'd beat her at her own game and Tracy Fudge was a hot Pony Club games player.

Penny put her thinking cap on.

The Horse of the Year Show, one of the biggest equestrian events in the world, was scheduled for the second week of October. The best horses from all over the world would be competing but they had to qualify at certain shows first.

The big Pony Club games finals, the Prince Philip Cup, was held at the Horse of the Year Show.

Tracy Fudge's team, The Ellington, had already qualified for this prestigious event at one of the Zone finals. That made her even smugger than usual. Only one Zone final remained now to be held at the Taunton Valley Pony Club headquarters in Somerset.

Pip, Dom, Carlos and Sam were cleaning grooming kit brushes in the wash room.

'I've got an idea,' said Penny as she came in carrying a bucket of muddy brushes. 'How about forming a games team and trying to qualify for the Prince Philip Cup? There are five of us. We all have good ponies. We could do it if we studied the rules and practised hard.'

The others thought this was a great idea.

'Let's call ourselves THE FETLOCKS HALL FLYERS,' said Sam.

They all agreed this would be a smashing name.

Penny went to ask Potty Smythe if they could compete.

The headmistress, who happened to be district commissioner of the Blackmud and Sparkling Vale Pony Club, agreed and offered to coach them herself.

'You really ought to be the Blackmud and Sparkling Vale B team,' she said, 'but you can call your team whatever you like. You'll have to get your skates on though because you must win at an area competition first to qualify for the Zone finals. If you win a Zone final your team qualifies for the Prince Philip Cup at H.O.Y.S.

'There's an Area competition at Darling Place next week and the last Zone finals are in three weeks' time.'

'Right,' said Penny. 'We'll be there!'

Training began the next day instead of their usual riding lessons. There was no time to lose. Potty Smythe, Henry and Ben Faloon marked out the correct size arena consisting of six lanes, one for each team. Each lane had a line of five bending poles, or tall tomato canes, for the ponies to weave in and out of. From the start line the competitors had to race to the 'change-over' line. Ponies that were not racing had to stand six metres back from these lines.

Most races required four ponies. Some needed five.

The Fetlocks Hall Flyers were Penny on Patch, Pip on Waggit, Sam on Landsman, Dom on Budget (his own dressage pony, Sir Fin, was too valuable to risk at games so he borrowed Budget, a retired polo pony from Fetlocks), and Carlos on Shilling (Budget's daughter, who was as quick and supple as her mother).

First they practised change-over technique at speed.

Potty Smythe handed Penny a show cane and told her to gallop as fast as possible to Pip, who was waiting to grab it at the change-over line.

'Always pass the cane from right hand to right hand,' instructed Potty. 'If you drop it you have to dismount, mount again and then pass it to your receiver.'

At first Waggit was scared of Patch charging full tilt at him with his rider leaning out holding a stick. He would not stand still, making it difficult for Pip to grab the cane from Penny.

'It's OK, Waggit,' shouted Patch as he sped up to him.

'Just stand still so Pip can grab the cane and be ready to shoot off when she says,' added Penny in Equalese.

Waggit did as he was told and soon became very good at it.

Next the team practised the Bending race by weaving their ponies in and out of the rows of tomato canes. They started off in trot but by the end of their training session they were galloping down them very neatly.

Carlos wanted to show everyone how he could mount and dismount from a pony at full gallop. It was a trick the gauchos on his father's ranch had taught him. He could also pick up a hat from the ground while riding at top speed and put it on his head.

Dom, with his perfect sense of balance, was soon copying him. They galloped side by side towards two hats, leaned down, grabbed them, swung back into the saddle and then placed the hats on each other's heads!

The three girls whooped and whistled. Potty, Henry and Ben cheered and clapped.

'It's not a bad team we have here at all,' laughed Ben Faloon. 'I've me money on them!'

On the other side of the hedge to the field where they were practising, Tracy Fudge on Hob and Jade Andrews on Firefly were hacking back from the woods. They were returning from a secret meeting with the Devlipeds.

'What the blazes are those little rubbish heads up to now?' snarled Tracy, standing up in her stirrups and looking over the hedge.

'Looks like they're training for mounted games. The Ellington might have a bit of competition,' hissed Jade between her thin little lips.

'No chance,' said Tracy Fudge, kicking Hob into a trot.

For the next few days The Fetlocks Hall Flyers practised the various events they would have to do at the Area competition until they were foot perfect.

Eight other teams were entered but only the best two would qualify for the Zone finals.

The morning of the Area games arrived. The

excited team and ponies travelled in two Fetlocks Hall lorries. Everyone was a bit nervous, except for Carlos, who said it would be a walkover.

On arrival the ponies, looking very fit, were unloaded, tacked up and ready for action. The Flyers joined the other teams for a quick practice in the field next to the arena. This gave them an opportunity to have a look at the opposition. It was obvious that their main competition was going to come from the Portmain Pony Club, who seemed to be more polished than the other teams. They were riding hard and out to qualify.

The teams were called over for the start. No time for nerves now.

The starter's flag went down and the first team riders were off for Event One, the Bending race. Pip and Waggit set a good pace but Penny and Patch (last to go) finished just behind a quick grey Portmain pony so The Portmain got that point.

The next race, Event Two, Ball and Cone, was won by Sam so the scores were one all.

'None of them will beat Carlos in the Stepping Stones race,' whispered Henry to Ben Faloon. 'The riders have to dismount and run along the top of six upturned buckets, mount again and gallop through the finish.'

Carlos, whose long legs together with his spectacular speed at remounting, made it look easy, won Event Three and put The Flyers in the lead again! Whoops of excitement came from their supporters.

The Blackmud and Sparkling Vale team won Event Four, the Tack Shop, but The Portmain won Event Five, the Old Sock, making them level with The Flyers!

The team was getting apprehensive now but Pip and Dom, who had been practising together, won the Rope (Event Six) by two lengths. Their ponies' strides matched exactly.

Not to be outdone, the Portmain Pony Club won the Two Mug (Event Seven), putting the rival teams level again!

Finally Dom clinched the competition by coming home first in Event Eight (the Five Flag race), finishing well ahead of the best Portmain pony.

The top three scores were:

The Fetlocks Hall Flyers 4 points
The Portmain Pony Club 3 points
The Blackmud and Sparkling Vale 1 point

The Flyers and their supporters went wild with excitement. Dom was being carried shoulder high around the collecting ring. The ponies were delighted too.

'WE WON!' Penny told them. 'You were all brilliant.'

'Will the first three teams please remount and come into the arena for the prize-giving,' said the announcer.

The teams lined up in front of the Judges' Box. Penny looked down the line of proud ponies and riders and grinned at the rest of her teammates, who all smiled back.

'And the winners of the Blackmud and Sparkling Vale Pony Club Area Games competition are ... THE PORTMAIN PONY CLUB. Will The Portmain come forward please?'

The Flyers thought their jaws would drop off. There must be some mistake.

The jubilant Portmain team punched the air and shouted a loud 'YES'!

'Second place goes to our new team THE FETLOCKS HALL FLYERS and third place to our own BLACKMUD AND SPARKLING VALE PONY CLUB. Well done, everybody. We will look forward to seeing our first and second prizewinners at the next Zone finals at the Taunton Valley.'

It was Lady Lavinia Darling who handed out the

rosettes. The Portmain led the rest of the teams around the arena in a lap of honour.

Once out of the ring the Flyers crowded around Potty Smythe, asking for an explanation.

'Well,' she said, 'it looked as though you had it in the bag until one of the parents called for a stewards' inquiry. Mrs Bean, Suzy Bean's mother from The Portmain, lodged an objection. She said she had proof that Sam had been across the change-over line on Landsman when receiving her flag from Penny in Event Eight. As the district commissioner I had to lodge the complaint with the Chief Steward, who agreed that Landsman did have one hoof over the line. That meant you were disqualified from the Five Flag Race and The Portmain were awarded the event. They took the point.

So the amended scores were:

The Portmain Pony Club 4 points
The Fetlocks Hall Flyers 3 points
The Blackmud and Sparkling Vale 1 point

'Now run along all of you and shake hands with the Portmain team. You must always show goodwill.'

They did as they were told. The Portmain were very sporting and said they looked forward to seeing them at the Zone finals.

Sam was not only hopping mad but felt bad about letting her team down.

'Any one of us could have done it,' said Pip and they all agreed.

'There will be no margin for error at the Zone finals,' said Potty Smythe.

'I'll do better next time,' promised Sam.

The day had certainly given them all something to think about. Being a team was great fun but carried with it responsibility to each other.

Landsman was upset that he had caused them to lose a point and be disqualified from the Five Flag race, but he could not be blamed as he did not know the rules. As Penny helped load him back into the lorry she told him he'd have to be more patient the next time. Poor Landsman didn't understand about the lines. He hung his head and looked very sad. He promised to do better the next time.

# CHAPTER TEN

# Fetlocks Hall
# For Ever

Late that night, when everybody was tucked up in bed, Penny crept out of her room and padded softly down the great staircase into the hall.

She twisted the wooden unicorn on the banisters at the base of the stairs. Antonia and Arabella Fitznicely floated down from their portraits.

'Dear Princess Penny, we have not had the opportunity to congratulate you on your coronation yet,' said the twins, making a dainty curtsy. 'Mama and Papa say you are truly one of our family now, so may we call you sister?'

Penny returned the curtsy and said she would be honoured to have them as sisters.

'Where are your parents tonight?' asked Penny, looking up at their empty portraits.

'Gone to a Ball at the Montecutes',' said Antonia.

'How did the Pony Club games go?' asked Arabella.

Penny told them what had happened blow by blow, including their humiliation at being disqualified in the last race. 'Landsman had no idea he should keep his feet behind that line,' she said.

'There will be a lot more competition at the Zone finals,' said Antonia. 'Would it not help to have a meeting with the ponies and teach them the rules of the games? I've been watching you all using those magic computer things in the library. The Pony Club must have its own website with film clips of ponies competing in the Prince Philip Cup. Could you not borrow a computer, take it down to the stable yard, and show the ponies some films so that they might learn from it?'

'Oh, Antonia,' cried Arabella. 'You are the cleverest of sisters!'

Penny agreed with her.

She unplugged one of the laptops from a desk in the library. She carried it down to the yard with the twins floating along behind.

As they passed Tracy Fudge's lorry Penny noticed that strange rubbery burning smell again.

'Devlipeds,' said Arabella, twitching her nose like a mouse. 'There's something bad going on there.'

Penny explained to the twins how she had already seen the Devlipeds plotting with the Pony Brats the morning after her coronation and how they planned to make them Devliped Prince and Princesses once they passed their A tests.

'That's disgusting!' said Antonia.

'Shocking!' said Arabella.

Penny described her plan to get the Pony Brats to leave Fetlocks of their own accord so that they did not sit their A tests in the spring.

'I was lucky with Benjamin,' she said. 'It was so fortunate that Carlos bashed his ear.'

'We know,' said Arabella. 'We saw it all – most amusing and so clever of you, Penny.'

'I'm planning to get Tracy Fudge to go next,' said Penny. 'That's why it's so important we win the Prince Philip Cup. I think she'll be so miffed when we beat her at her own game she'll never live it down at Fetlocks Hall or in the Pony Club. She's such a spoilt brat she'll have a screaming fit and leave. Tracy already knows we have a good team and she may try to stop us getting to the finals. I need you to watch her and Jade like hawks and keep me informed of anything suspicious. Would you do that for me?

'Of course we will,' said Antonia.

'We are all sisters now, after all,' added Arabella, squeezing her hand.

'And *we* have the added advantage of being invisible to them,' laughed Antonia.

Penny took Patch, Waggit, Landsman, Budget and Shilling into the barn to show them some Pony Club games star performers on www.pcuk.org. Antonia found the website for her and downloaded the Rule Book.

The ponies loved the film and stared at the screen with huge eyes.

They all agreed it would be easy for them to copy the manoeuvres but they did find it hard to take in the Rule Book.

'Well,' said Penny, 'you'll just have to trust your riders and do exactly as they say.'

They all agreed.

After Penny's computer session with the ponies their

performance was perfect.

The children could not believe the improvement. Potty Smythe had a pretty good idea that Penny had been coaching them in some way but kept quiet.

The day of the Zone finals arrived. The two lorries, carrying ponies and children and driven by Ben Faloon and Henry, set off very early in the morning for Taunton.

There were only four Zone finals. The winners from each final qualified for H.O.Y.S. There were two runners-up competitions, from which the best two teams went through. That made up the six teams for the Prince Philip Cup.

The Taunton Valley Zone final had fifteen teams entered including the Portmain Pony Club, the Flyers' main rivals and hot favourites to win.

'There are a lot of good teams to beat today,' said Potty Smythe, 'so let's all do our best. Ride straight and true with determination. I know you will always be fair and abide by the rules because you are brave Fetlocks children. Good luck, everyone!'

Penny gave the ponies a similar briefing.

'Everything depends on you ponies,' she said. 'Obey your riders, balance them when they lean over to one side. Stop, go, turn and bend. Help them by aiming for the flag containers. Don't miss any bending poles. Stay behind the change-over line until the exchange is completed. Gallop as fast as you can but above all take care of your riders.'

'We will, Princess Penny,' the five ponies replied.

The teammates made a circle. Penny reached her hand into the centre and the others all piled a hand on top, then thrust them up into the air.

'Fetlocks Hall for ever!' they cheered.

The day was not easy. After six events The Flyers were exhausted. Pip had fallen off a stepping stone and sprained her ankle. She bravely completed the course but her foot was so swollen Dom had to cut her boot off to bandage it. Obviously she could not continue. They were one team member down but still had the required four. Pip said she'd be OK as Number Five in the last race as that did not involve riding.

The Portmain were top of the leader board with The Southwest Down second and The Flyers lying third.

Then Carlos triumphed at the Sword, being easily the fastest rider over the line with all four rings on his sword.

Dom was unbeatable at the Sharpshooters and

Penny and Patch outran the other teams in the Postman's.

The Flyers were now lying equal with The Portmain and badly needed one point to win. Everything depended on the last Fishing race. Penny called a quick team conference.

'We've been here before,' she said. 'We need to win this race with no mistakes. Sam, you are last to go so make sure Landsman stays behind the changeover line until Pip hangs your fish on the hook. Then gallop as fast as you can and outrun The Portmain's Number Four rider.'

Sam gritted her teeth and nodded. Her stomach was churning but she did not let it show.

Penny knew Landsman felt the same. She whispered a word of encouragement to him as he stood shaking behind the start line.

Penny and Patch lined up with the other Number One riders. She tightly gripped her cane with its cup hook on the end for catching the fish. Her eyes were homed in on the litter bin on the centre line containing the plastic fish.

The starter's flag went down. With her cane and hook poised she and Patch shot towards to the litter bin.

Patch deftly stopped for a second while Penny

hooked a fish and galloped on towards Pip (who stood holding a cross post with hooks screwed to the underside) three metres behind the change-over line. Pip, standing almost on one leg now because of her injured ankle, grabbed Penny's fish and hung it on a hook as Patch circled around her, carefully staying behind the change-over line as he did this. As soon as the fish was secured on the cross post, Penny shot back to the finish line. She could see the Number One Portmain pony just ahead of her. Dom was waiting to take her fishing rod, his right hand outstretched.

The crowd was cheering them on madly but Penny could not hear a thing. All she knew was The Portmain's Number One rider had just beaten her at the change-over. Dom and Budget were brilliant. Knowing she had to catch up and overtake the Portmain pony, Budget used all her old polo skills. Dom was so perfectly balanced he did not even stop to hook his fish. Budget slowed down just a fraction so that he could take aim at one, and then sped towards Pip.

'Catch it, I'm not stopping!' shouted Dom.

And he didn't. As Budget did one of her perfect polo turns, Pip took the fish off Dom's hook and hung it up. Dom was halfway up the course and in front of The Portmain.

Carlos was waiting for the perfect change-over. He grabbed the cane from Dom and set off for the bin. He was a little slower at hooking the fish but very fast returning.

Sam was waiting with Landsman at the start line. Landsman was counting down to himself as he watched Shilling speed towards him. He was standing perfectly still like a live wire waiting for action.

The Portmain Number Three and Carlos were neck and neck at the change-over. Sam took the cane from Carlos. Landsman leapt forward into a gallop. With her eyes on the bin Sam sped down the course and hooked a fish just in front of her rival. Then, cane outstretched, she aimed at Pip, who grabbed the fish and hung it up. Landsman, careful not to cross the line, was a little slow to take off for the finish. The Portmain pony was a length ahead!

'COME ON, LANNIE,' cried Sam, digging her heels into her pony's sides.

Landsman laid his ears back and sped up to the galloping pony to beat him by a nose across the finish line!

The games were over. All the teams lined up in the arena for the official results.

The Flyers should be the winners but what would

happen if another objection had been lodged?

They were not home yet and the team knew it. They looked nervously at one another. Penny crossed her fingers.

'And the winners are ... THE FETLOCKS HALL FLYERS,' came the announcement.

'What a great performance. We look forward to seeing you all at H.O.Y.S.'

The Flyers had won the Zone finals and qualified for the Horse of the Year Show!

Everyone went mad. They hugged the ponies, hugged each other and hugged the other teams.

Poor Pip's ankle was really painful but she refused to be left out of the limelight. Carlos led her pony and Dom hoisted her up behind him on Budget, where she clung round his waist as the team galloped around the ring on their lap of honour.

The only person who was not ecstatic about their performance was Tracy Fudge, who had heard about the whole thing before they got home. Mandy Fitch's mum, one of the Ellington mothers, had been there. She'd phoned her daughter with news of this new dangerous team. Mandy Fitch had phoned Tracy.

Tracy Fudge was spitting nails.

# CHAPTER ELEVEN

# The Horse of the Year Show

A big banner made from an old sheet was pinned up on the rusty gates at the entrance to Fetlocks Hall. It had coloured balloons sailing from it and big red letters saying, 'WELL DONE, THE FETLOCKS HALL FLYERS'.

All the staff and children of Fetlocks Hall lined the drive to cheer in the two school lorries containing the triumphant team. Penny and Potty Smythe could see the Fitznicelys sitting on the gates, waving as they drove in.

The ponies were unloaded and given extra carrots and apples in their feeds. Penny thanked them all for being so brilliant.

'What happens next?' said Patch.

'We all go to Birmingham in October for six days of competitions at the Horse of the Year Show.'

'Whoopee!' said the ponies. 'Here's to us! Ponies of the Year!'

Penny called her parents to tell them the good news. Potty Smythe was going to arrange free tickets for them for the last day of the finals.

Dom's parents were coming up from Cornwall for the whole show in their camper van.

Carlos's father was flying over to coach the Brazilian Showjumping Team. He went into cheers of delight when Carlos told him he would also be competing.

Pip and Sam felt lonely and left out as they had no families to share their success story with.

Pip burst into tears when Dom told her his parents were staying for the week.

He gave her a huge hug and said that as he did not

have any sisters he'd be proud to share his parents with her. She cried even more!

Sam said she had Landsman for her family and she couldn't get better than that.

The next month seemed to go very quickly. There was a huge amount of preparation to get five ponies and children ready to leave for a week at the National Exhibition Centre.

Tracy Fudge went home for two weeks prior to the show to practise with her team.

Jade Andrews had qualified Firefly for the J.A. (top junior) Showjumping Championships at the show so she had gone for special training with Andrew Sailwell, Olympic Showjumping gold medallist, in Surrey.

The team practised hard. Scholarship children had so much mucking out and strenuous yard work to do that they were always very fit. Carlos and Dom did practise some weight training though. Ben Faloon showed them the Irish method by picking up an anvil and running across the yard with it!

Three weeks, two weeks, one week to go and the clock was ticking fast.

The whole school was coming to the show at various intervals and they planned to have a full house of supporters for the final day of the championships. The Fitznicelys were haunting as well. They had some ancestors at Packlington Hall, very near to the Exhibition Centre, so they arranged to stay with them.

The children started packing the lorry two days before the show with everything they would need for the week. Potty Smythe drove the Land Rover up with an extra trailer attached full of supplies. Mrs Dogberry had ironed a new sweatshirt and pair of jodhpurs for each day. The new shirts were navy blue with a rearing silver unicorn on the front and the name of the team in silver stars on the back.

Penny paid a visit to the secret hiding place on the front steps to pick up her little silver vial of Unicorn Tears, just in case there were any injuries while they were away.

Finally, the excited ponies were loaded and the lorries set off on the long trip to the show. They would be staying in temporary show stables while their riders had packed their sleeping bags for the bunks in the lorries.

All wagons had to be checked for security before they could be let into the National Exhibition Centre. Once clear, the attendant vet checked the identity of each pony from its passport before they were allocated their stables for the week.

Ben and Henry parked the lorries.

'Jade Andrews and Tracy Fudge are parked side by side over there,' said Sam, pointing across the lorry park.

The games teams were all stabled in block three. In the row opposite the Fetlocks team there was a sign saying, 'The Ellington Pony Club'.

'Too close for comfort,' said Penny as she checked the name of the stable facing hers. It said 'Tracy Fudge, Hob'.

A tall, dark, handsome man came running over to the Fetlocks lorries.

It was Don Frederico Cavello, Carlos's father. Carlos jumped out and slapped palms with him, laughing and joking in Portuguese.

Dom's parents, Willum and Georgie Trelawney, had arrived too. They were in the caravan park preparing a barbecue for everybody.

Once the ponies were all comfortable, everyone piled over there and helped themselves to sausages, burgers, Cornish pasties, steaks, salad, hot buttered rolls and cakes and trifles.

Dom's parents were very pleased to meet everyone, especially Pip.

'We've heard lots about you, young lady,' said his

mum, handing her a plate.

'Hope your ankle's good now,' said his dad.

Pip nodded, her mouth full of burger.

Don Cavello brought his Showjumping team over. The Trelawneys got their guitars out and played some flamenco music. The team gave a mad display of dancing and everyone joined in.

It was huge fun and everyone had a great evening but Potty Smythe made sure the five children were away and checking the ponies by 8 p.m. and everyone was in bed by 9 p.m.

They had a hard week ahead.

The first three days of the Prince Philip Cup was a warm-up competition with prizes for all the six teams.

The serious competition was held over the following three days. The prestigious final would be held on the last night of the show and carried double points to add to their scores.

The other teams competing were: The Ellington, The Oaklees, The Baddingsworth, The Fernie Foxes and The Blazers (from Northern Ireland).

At the end of the warm-up competition The Blazers were clearly the leaders with The Ellington second, Fernie Foxes third, Fetlocks Hall Flyers fourth, Oaklees fifth and The Baddingsworth sixth.

'I know they are really polished teams,' Potty Smythe said encouragingly, 'but you still have a good chance to catch up over the next three days, so kick on, chaps!'

Penny talked to the ponies to keep their spirits up.

'Those Irish ponies are dead nippy,' said Waggit. That roan one with half an ear missing and a parrot mouth is dynamite!'

'Hob is giving us the evil eye,' said Landsman. 'He threatened to kick me yesterday during my change-over.'

'That's elimination as well if he does and Tracy will know it,' added Penny. 'He's only trying to frighten you.'

Jade Andrews was in the J.A. jump-off that night so the team went to watch. The jumps were huge and decorated with brilliantly coloured trays of flowers and fancy wings. There were nine ponies in the jump-off. The fastest clear round would win.

Firefly came prancing in, covered in sweat. She flew round clear until the very last double where she got too keen as usual and just rolled the last pole, giving her four faults. A great *OOOOhhh* went up from the crowd.

Jade was furious. She knew she would be eliminated for giving Firefly a beating in public but everyone could see she wanted to.

She dismounted in the tunnel and threw the reins to her groom without even giving her pony a second look.

She joined Tracy Fudge in the wings to watch the next round.

Jade ended up sixth. She made a huge fuss about going into the ring to collect her prize because it was not a first. Finally, her instructor picked her up and threw her on to Firefly, giving the pony a slap on the bottom to make sure his horrid little pupil got into the arena before anyone noticed her tantrum.

The next three days were crucial for the team. Penny had bitten her nails so low it hurt to groom Patch. The ponies had all been given an extra feed of competition mix to perk them up.

The first afternoon performance went very well. Don Cavello was watching his son as he wheeled his pony round, gaucho style, reaching for the lowest point so that he could accurately aim the socks into their containers in the Old Sock race. He clapped wildly as Carlos won each of his events.

The Flyers finished on a really good score that moved them up into third place.

The next day the Irish team had a mishap. The grey Connemara pony was going so fast he could not stop. He smashed into the boards at the end of the arena. The pony was OK but his rider, Liam O'Hara, went sailing over his head and landed among the spectators. He hit the back of his head on a metal seat and was rushed to hospital with concussion. Then Siobhan Murphy caught her foot in her partner's stirrup leather during the Rope Race and tore a ligament.

That meant they were minus two riders and were out of the competition!

The poor things had come so far. Everybody was really sorry for them. The Irish team were remarkably good-natured about the whole thing. Lots of the competitors went to see Liam in hospital that night. He had been unconscious for an hour and had a bad cut on the back of his neck, but he was going to be fine.

So that left The Ellington in the lead by two points with The Flyers lying second!

The tension was growing. No one in the Fetlocks Hall lorries got much sleep that night.

\* \* \*

All the time Tracy Fudge had been opposite Penny in the stable area she had not said a word. The other members of the Ellington team were really nice and very sporting. They always wished the other teams good luck before a performance and would be pleased to lend a brush or a bucket to anyone. They were too professional to mention it but Penny guessed they all disliked Tracy as much as anyone else. She just happened to have the best and most experienced games pony even though he was very bad-tempered. She also rode very well.

Penny did not trust her one little bit.

On the morning of the big day, Penny went down to feed the ponies with Henry at 6 a.m.

They noticed none of the ponies were looking out over their doors, waiting for breakfast.

Penny heard no morning greetings, just heavy snoring.

To their amazement all the ponies were lying down fast asleep!

'Get up, Patch!' Penny shouted into the little skewbald pony's ear.

Patch slowly opened one eye, yawned and closed it again.

Penny shook Patch, who eventually yawned again and mumbled, 'Good morning.'

'Whatever is the matter with you, Patch?' asked Penny. 'For goodness' sake, wake up. We've got a big day ahead.'

'I'm sorry, Pen,' he said sleepily. 'I'm so tired. I don't think I can be ridden today.'

With that he dozed off again with his head on her knee.

This was terrible news. The final of the Prince Philip Cup was that evening and the ponies had to be on top form.

Penny was sitting in the stable with a snoring Patch, wondering what to do next, when Antonia and Arabella floated in through the wall.

As promised they had been keeping an eye on Tracy and Jade. They had glided over from Packlington Hall to the show lorry park last night when all the children, except the two Pony Brats, were at the hospital visiting Liam. They had seen the Brats in Jade's lorry, secretly sticking little yellow pills into mints. At dawn they had spotted them feeding the mints to the Fetlocks ponies!

'We don't know what these are but we found one in the straw in Patch's stable,' said Antonia, handing Penny a mint with a small yellow pill inserted into it.

Penny recognised the pill to be a tranquillizer, well known for making ponies drowsy.

'They've doped them, the little rats!' said Penny, boiling with anger. 'If the official vets find out we will be disqualified! I bet Jade and Tracy are on their way to tell them right now!'

In fact Henry had already called the vet. She was worried about the ponies' unusual behaviour.

Penny knew if doping was suspected the vet would do a blood test on the ponies. If it proved positive for any forbidden substance The Flyers would be thrown out of the competition!

Penny had no time to lose. She took the little silver vial of Unicorn Tears out of her pocket and trickled a drop on to Patch's tongue. She had no idea if it would work. It had the power of instant healing but she didn't know if it would cure ponies who had been doped.

She could hear Henry talking to the vet.

'Sounds like they've had a tranquillizer . . .' he was saying. 'If the blood tests prove positive the ponies cannot run tonight, of course.'

Penny looked at Patch. He was still lying in his thick golden straw snoring. The official show vet was only a few metres away carrying a syringe!

She had one thing left to try.

'*Let's Fly!*' she shouted in Equalese.

The combination of the Unicorn Tears and the

flying command worked. Patch suddenly shot up into the air and waggled his legs about. This seemed to wake him up and get him moving.

Penny told him to come down quickly and that the vet was going to stick a needle in him in a second so to stand still and be brave.

She quickly let herself out of the stable, bumping into the vet and Henry.

'He seems much better now,' she said as she darted into the next stable.

She did the same thing to the other four Fetlocks ponies and it worked just as well.

Henry was surprised the ponies had all recovered so quickly but the results of the blood tests would not be available until late that afternoon at the earliest. They were not allowed to ride the ponies unless the results were clear. That meant no badly needed morning practice and little time, if any, to warm up. Portia Manning-Smythe and the rest of the team were hopping mad when Henry told them what had happened and that the vet suspected the ponies had been doped. The children were hoping against hope that the tests would be negative. It would be devastating to have had such good luck so far only to be foiled in the final furlong like this.

Just then Penny's entire family turned up. Penny

hadn't seen them for so long and had missed them more than she could say. Although she was overjoyed to see them she could not forget the doping crisis. She blurted out the awful news that someone had tried to sabotage their hopes of winning by tranquillizing the ponies. They were all horrified at what had happened.

Were they competing that evening for the Prince Philip Cup or would they be disqualified?

It all seemed so unfair.

The ponies too were wondering what had happened. They told Penny that they had no idea the mints were not ordinary ones, though they had tasted a bit funny. About an hour after eating the mints they all felt very sleepy.

'I'm sure we will be able to compete tonight,' said Patch. 'We feel quite normal now.'

That was what Penny wanted to hear. She only hoped the laboratory vets thought the same thing.

The evening performance and finals started at 6 p.m. All teams had to declare and be inspected by 5 p.m.

The ponies were tacked up and ready to go. The children were nervously waiting outside their stables for the vets' verdict.

Don Frederico was furious. He paced up and

down, throwing his hands up into the air and muttering in Portuguese. The other parents said they would lodge an objection if the tests were positive. Of course, only Penny, the ponies and the Fitznicely twins knew who had done it.

The ponies were outraged.

'Even though we haven't had a warm-up,' said Shilling, 'we've got to show that Tracy Fudge and Jade Andrews that they just can't go around doping ponies.'

'We ARE going to run,' said Patch, 'and we ARE GOING TO WIN!'

They all agreed. THIS WAS WAR.

Potty Smythe's mobile went at 4.45 p.m.

'YES!' she yelled and everybody snapped into action.

Penny gave a huge sigh of relief. The blood tests were negative. The cure had worked.

They were ready to rumble!

Potty ran down to the collecting ring to declare the team fit to run. The steward in charge of the tack inspection passed them all in the nick of time.

As the riders lined up for the first race the crowd went wild.

Penny and Patch were first to run. In the lane next to her was Tracy Fudge on Hob.

She went bright red as Penny glared at her but the starter's flag was up. The ponies were tense and ready. Down came the flag . . . They were off like bullets.

Penny and Patch galloped up the bending poles like rockets. Neck and neck with Hob, Patch put on an extra spurt and beat him over the finish line.

'Two points, The Fetlocks Hall Flyers!' yelled the announcer.

The whole school had turned up on the last night. A huge view holla and whoops of delight went up from the Fetlocks crew.

Event Two, Ball and Cone, was next. Pip's ball fell off the far cone so she had to remount and pick it up, losing valuable time. The Oaklees won that race.

In Event Three, Stepping Stones, Carlos was unbelievable, running along the top of the upturned buckets with Shilling cantering loose alongside. He leapt straight off the last bucket on to Shilling, without slowing down.

Don Frederico shouted, 'Viva Brazilia!' and hugged Potty Smythe.

'Two points to The Fetlocks Hall Flyers,' shouted the announcer. 'That puts them in the lead!'

The crowd went crazy.

The Ellington won Event Four, Tack Shop, putting the two teams level again. But the great combination of Dom and Pip in the Rope race and fifth event put them back on top.

The Baddingsworth won Event Six, the Two Mug.

The Ellington won Event Seven, the Five Flag, bringing their score level with The Flyers again.

The next race was the 'Spare Event' in which the two leading teams went head to head.

This was the Two Flag race, for four riders only. Sam was reserve rider for this race and would take over if any of her team were injured.

Penny looked along the line of Fetlocks ponies. They all looked back at her.

'Come on, ponies,' she said. 'It's down to you now. WE CAN WIN THIS!'

Penny as Number One team rider and Pip as Number Three stood with their ponies at the start/finish line. Dom and Carlos, riders Two and Four, stood at the change-over line. Level with the first and fourth bending poles were two flag holders. The holder nearest the change-over end contained a flag while the other was empty.

Holding a flag in one hand, Penny waited for the signal. The starter's flag went down and she and Patch raced off towards the first holder. At full gallop she leaned over and neatly placed her flag in it. Patch went flat out towards the second holder. Penny whipped out the flag, expertly keeping her speed. She passed it to Dom at the change-over line. Dom grabbed the flag and raced back to the empty holder nearest him. He quickly placed his flag in it and sped on to pluck the flag from the next holder and pass it to Pip waiting at the start line. She repeated the exercise, hurtling down to Carlos, who was waiting eagerly at the change-over line. It all depended on him to beat the Ellington team back to the finish line. They were six lanes away so he could not see how they were doing. In fact The Ellington were in trouble. Tracy Fudge had knocked over the flag container. That meant she had to dismount, stand it up again, mount, insert the flag and then continue. The Ellington had lost serious time and were way behind.

Carlos, unaware of their misfortune, just went as fast as he could. Shilling was amazing. They galloped through the finish at top speed with Carlos carrying the last flag far in advance of the other team.

It was a sensational win.

The National Exhibition Centre had never heard such a din. It even woke up the Fitznicelys' ancestors at Packlington Hall across the road! The Earl of

Elham fell out of his portrait.

The teams lined up for the prize-giving with The Ellington next to The Flyers. Tracy Fudge was glaring daggers at Penny. Hob stood with his ears flat back. He knew he would be blamed for Tracy's mistake in the last race.

The atmosphere, as they waited for the official result, was electric. The audience fell silent.

'And the winners of the Prince Philip Cup are THE FETLOCKS HALL FLYERS!' yelled the announcer. 'Let's hear it for them!'

The crowd cheered madly as the team came forward for their prize. Everyone clapped in time to the music as The Flyers galloped around the ring five abreast, with Penny and Sam in the middle holding up the big silver cup with its ribbons flying. The lights went down. The spotlights were on them. They galloped down the centre line with their trophy to the roar of thousands of spectators and out through the tunnel.

'We owe all this to you guys,' said Penny to her team of triumphant ponies.

'We've had the time of our lives,' said Patch, 'but can we go home for some grass now? We'd like to be turned out in our big grassy park for a while.'

'You've all deserved a well-earned rest and the

juiciest grass in Dorset,' said Penny, scratching him behind his ear.

Tracy Fudge was really mad. She said the mistake was all Hob's fault and he was getting too old to be a top games pony any more.

'I want him sold to the knacker man!' she raged at her parents.

'Yes, Trace. You'll get a new pony for Christmas,' said her mother.

Potty Smythe overheard this and was outraged. She wrote Mrs Fudge a cheque for five hundred pounds for Hob.

'That's what you would have got for him from the knacker man,' she growled. 'He comes home with us tonight.'

However, something had not gone according to Penny's plan.

Tracy Fudge had *not*, as expected, had a tantrum for being beaten and given up. Penny was really worried now.

The Fitznicely twins were waiting for her in Patch's stable. She told them she had a sinking feeling her plan had not worked.

The twins had a brilliant idea.

'Go and tell Tracy what we saw,' they said. 'Let her

know, if she does not volunteer to leave Fetlocks Hall, that you'll tell Cherry Goodhart, the chairman of the Pony Club, what she and Jade did to the ponies. She'll be thrown out of the Club and never be able to ride for them again.'

So, after the celebrations at the Trelawneys' camper, Penny and the twins sneaked up on Tracy Fudge as she was watching Jade take part in another competition.

Of course Tracy denied everything but she went bright red when Penny produced the drug-stuffed mint the twins had given her.

'Now wouldn't Miss Goodhart like to know about this?' said Penny, holding it in front of her nose.

Tracy did not come back to Fetlocks after the show.

Some days later Tracy's parents phoned the head-mistress to inform her they had taken her out of school and she was going to St Handsome's College, another pony school in Yorkshire.

'Poor them!' said Penny, delighted that her plan to get the second Pony Brat out of Fetlocks had worked eventually – even if it did have a bit of a twist to it in the end.

# CHAPTER TWELVE

# A Dangerous Encounter

Any pupil sitting their A test at Fetlocks Hall had monthly assessments, which they had to pass in order to sit the exam. Jade Andrews, the only remaining potential A student, thought she was on to a good thing now that Benjamin and Tracy had left because she would get all the instructors' attention and was sure to pass. With the help of the

Devlipeds she alone would be in charge of Fetlocks Hall once they had gained control by defeating the unicorns.

However, Jade was a lazy girl and never seemed to do any studying for the exam. She spent a lot of time in her big shiny lorry, watching television and playing computer games.

Yet somehow she passed every assessment with flying colours. Everybody suspected her of cheating but nobody had any evidence.

Jade's next assessment was to take place at the end of term just before the school broke up for Christmas. The questions were set by the 'management' or previous A students under the guidance of Potty Smythe.

Penny thought it was going to be a hard task to get Jade Andrews to leave.

There was only one week to go until Jade sat her last assessment before she took the A test next term. Penny was racking her brains for a plan to get rid of her, but so far no luck.

That evening Penny was in the library doing her homework. She was all alone with a book called *Know Your Horse*, when Antonia and Arabella floated up.

'We've got some disturbing news,' said Arabella as they settled down on either side of her. 'We *know* Jade Andrews is a cheat. Last night we saw her sneak out to her lorry and go to the cooker in its living area. The oven was not turned on and she certainly was not looking for fairy cakes. We saw her take out some papers and read them. When we went back later for a closer look we found they were stolen exam papers. That's how she passes her assessments without doing any work.'

'I wonder how she's getting them?' said Penny.

'Devlipeds are very clever,' said Antonia. 'What happens if one has stolen the assessment questions and answers from the safe in Miss Manning-Smythe's office and is secretly teaching them to Jade Andrews?'

Penny gasped! 'That means they are actually getting into the school!'

'Unicorn Princesses have to be vigilant and keep Devlipeds out of Terestequinus,' said Arabella.

'You are going to have to see the creature off!' said Antonia.

Penny was really nervous this time. She did not like the idea of coming face to face with a Devliped again.

She remembered how effective the Lance of Courage was when taming the Devliped she rode during her test. It must be able to fend them off. It was only of any use to an acting Unicorn Princess. Only Penny had the power to use it. The twins were retired Unicorn Princesses and although they had used one during their reign they were not empowered to do so now. She'd have to lie in wait for the Devliped and fight it all alone.

She thought it best to keep the Lance handy for these next few days so she collected it from its secret hiding place beneath the step and stuck it into the waistband of her school skirt. For some reason Queen Stardust's Horn jumped up too and tucked itself in between her blazer buttons.

The day before the end-of-term assessment came and there was no sign of Devlipeds. Maybe Arabella and Antonia had been wrong. Penny was feeling desperate. Whatever could she do?

Then Patch saved the day.

Penny was emptying a wheelbarrow with a mucking-out fork that afternoon when she heard him call from the field.

He was pacing up and down on the other side of the fence from the lorry park, looking very agitated.

'It smells funny over there, Penny,' he shouted. Ponies have a very sensitive sense of smell. 'I think the Jademobile is on fire!' Penny dropped her fork and ran over to the lorry. Patch was right. No mistaking the faint smell of burning rubber.

Taking the silver cane from the waistband of her jeans, she crept silently up the steps to the lorry and opened the door.

She could not see a Devliped anywhere. Then she remembered what the twins had said about the hiding place. Holding her little silver cane in one hand, she turned the handle on the oven door.

To her horror the door exploded open and a small Devliped shot out at her like a rocket!

It knocked the cane out of her hand. Without it she was powerless. It lay between her and the snarling Devliped. Every time she reached out for the cane the Devliped sent a jet of flames from its nostrils, preventing her from getting close to it.

She thought she was done for. Her only chance was to blow Queen Stardust's Horn and see if it helped in any way.

Quickly she pulled it out of her shirt buttons and blew into it. The effect was dramatic. The Devliped obviously did not like the sound. It shook its head violently, momentarily deflecting its flames away from Penny's hand and the cane. There was just enough time for her to grab it.

Instantly it transformed itself into a long shining lance with a sharp spear on the end. Blue flashes spurted from it. Penny held on tightly to the shaft with both hands.

The Devliped screamed and disappeared in a puff of blue smoke!

The burning spear became a little silver cane again. She tucked it back into her waistband. She thanked the Golden Horn for coming with her and put it back between her buttons. Penny found a folder in the oven. It contained the stolen assessment questions and answers. She had obviously caught the Devliped while he was delivering them to the secret hiding place for Jade to read before the exam.

She gave the folder to Henry, saying she had found it on the muck heap.

Henry was stunned by her find and returned it to the office.

Surprisingly enough, when Jade Andrews sat her end-of-term assessment the next day she failed miserably.

Of course this meant it would be impossible now for her to become an A student. She would never become a Devliped Princess so there was no point in her being at Fetlocks. If the school found out she'd been cheating in all her previous assessments she'd be in huge trouble so Jade asked her parents to take her out of Fetlocks and send her to finishing school in Switzerland.

Penny was delighted that Jade and the rest of the Pony Brats had left Fetlocks Hall for ever. Thanks to her, Terrestequinus was safe for the time being.

She secretly gave herself a pat on the back but knew she could not have done it without the help of all her friends and, of course, the precious ponies.

## CHAPTER THIRTEEN

# Home for Christmas

The last day of the autumn term came.

There had been a light fall of snow in the night, dusting the great house with its twinkling windows. Fetlocks Hall looked even more magical in its petticoat of snow.

Penny was looking forward to seeing her family again for the Christmas holidays but she was heartbroken to leave the ponies and her new friends.

'It's only four weeks,' said Patch as Penny wiped

away a stray tear with his long mane. 'The staff will still be here over the holiday to look after us. Henry will see to that.'

'But I will miss you so,' sobbed Penny, wrapping her arms round his brown and white neck.

She was all packed and ready to be picked up by Bunty Bevan and her family in the old red Land Rover.

'I've got something for you for Christmas, Patch,' Penny said, fumbling in her pocket. 'You can't eat it until Christmas Day.'

She pulled out a stocking, which she had made from an old pair of tights. It was stuffed with apples and carrots and mints.

'Yummy!' said Patch. 'You'd better give it to Henry for my Christmas dinner or I'll eat it all up now!'

As Penny walked out of Patch's stable all the ponies' heads appeared over their doors.

'Merry Christmas, Princess Penny,' they all shouted together.

'And a very Merry Christmas everyone,' said Penny, curtsying in the snowy yard.

Penny had asked if Sam and Pip would like to come home with her for Christmas. Mrs Simms had agreed it would be a wonderful idea as they had no families of their own.

'I've promised to stay here and help look after the ponies over the holiday but thanks awfully anyway,' said Sam.

'Dom's invited me down to Cornwall,' blushed Pip.

'Let's have a party back at school in the New Year,' said Penny. 'I'm sure Potty Smythe will agree. I'm not sure I can stand being away from you lot and the ponies for a month. The Christmas holidays are so long here.'

They all agreed this was a smashing idea.

Carlos was going back to Brazil for Christmas but he said he would email them all over the holidays.

Potty Smythe had a real Christmas present for everyone with the news that Jade's parents had phoned to say she was not coming back to Fetlocks Hall.

Henry had the best news ever. Peter Fitzcannon, her favourite vet, had broken up with his girlfriend, Lavinia Darling, and had invited her to the Hunt Ball!

The Fitznicely family were looking forward to a good haunting over Christmas. They usually visited all their other ghostly friends on Christmas Eve and got up to all kinds of scary pranks. The twins said they would miss their dear sister Penny too much and could not wait for the party in the New Year at Fetlocks.

Potty Smythe stood with Penny at the top of the steps.

'I'll look after all our secrets, Penny,' she whispered. 'Even a Unicorn Princess must have a holiday sometime, you know.'

The old red Land Rover swung in between the gates and scrunched to a halt by the front entrance.

The door opened and Ollie jumped out.

'Penny, Penny, Ollie ride ponies!' he shouted.

Everyone laughed. He was dressed in a cowboy suit complete with lasso and Stetson hat.

The whole family tumbled out of the car. Mr Simms picked up his daughter and gave her a big kiss on the cheek.

She'd forgotten how much she had missed them all.

'Thanks so much for taking care of her,' said Mrs Simms to Potty Smythe.

'Not at all,' replied the headmistress with a twinkle in her eye. 'She has been taking care of us!'

Hugs and hearty slaps on the back were exchanged between Bunty Bevan and Potty Smythe.

The terriers and the deerhounds exchanged greetings.

Penny's team mates, the Fitznicely family, Potty Smythe, Henry and Ben Faloon stood between two watchful stone unicorns and waved goodbye to Penny.

As the Land Rover moved off leaving tyre marks in the snow, Penny looked back at Fetlocks Hall.

At first glance, it looked like a snowstorm was coming but the flakes turned into a flurry of shining white unicorns with King Valentine himself in the lead.

They whirled round the car, tossing their long silver manes and beating their wings.

'Well done, Princess Penny,' they called. 'SEE YOU NEXT TERM!'

'Looks like we're in for some snow,' said Mr Simms.

*Not quite the end!*

# More frolics from Fetlocks Hall . . .

Fetlocks Hall is in trouble and may have to close! How will Penny save the school!?!

# Glitterwings Academy:
## Where Fairies Flourish!

To visit the most glimmery and glittery fairy school ever go to:
www.glitterwingsacademy.co.uk

# For more adventures with Madame Pamplemousse and Madeleine:

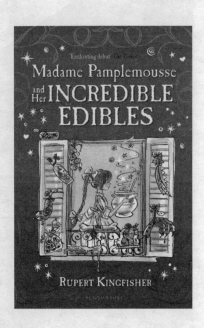

## Filled with delectable, irresistible and other-worldly delights